S

Bette Howell was born in ████████. Her father was a miner and her mother a teacher. She served as a radar operator with an anti-aircraft battery in the war. As a child she wrote stories and pantomimes to be acted out in the garden by a neighbourhood gang. Winning the *Mail on Sunday* Novel Competition in 1985 gave her the impetus to fulfil a lifelong ambition of becoming a full-time writer. Her second book, *Silver Riding*, continues the glorious adventures of May and Otley begun in *Wuthering Depths*. She now lives in Keighley, near Haworth.

BETTE HOWELL

SILVER RIDING

PENGUIN BOOKS

PENGUIN BOOKS

Published by the Penguin Group
27 Wrights Lane, London w8 5tz, England
Viking Penguin Inc., 40 West 23rd Street, New York, New York 10010, USA
Penguin Books Australia Ltd, Ringwood, Victoria, Australia
Penguin Books Canada Ltd, 2801 John Street, Markham, Ontario, Canada l3r 1b4
Penguin Books (NZ) Ltd, 182–190 Wairau Road, Auckland 10, New Zealand
Penguin Books Ltd, Registered Offices: Harmondsworth, Middlesex, England

First published 1991
1 3 5 7 9 10 8 6 4 2

Made and printed in Great Britain by
Richard Clay Ltd, Bungay, Suffolk
Filmset in 10/12 pt Monophoto Baskerville

For Richard and Edyta

A DESPERATE SUN stabbed a hole in the drizzle as I made my way down to the Citadel for our Common Market butter. Instinctively I hid behind my umbrella in case somebody recognized me, but I needn't have worried because everybody was doing the same.

A long line of wet Pakistanis, unmarried mothers and old-age pensioners straggled out into the main road and round the multi-storey car park. The Sally Army, used to dealing with down and outs, got through us at the speed of light.

'How many in the family?' inquired the captain pleasantly.

I was tempted to say fifteen, like the woman in front of me, but I didn't want to risk having a heart attack eating fifteen pounds of butter. In fact, I didn't really want any butter at all as I'm on a diet, but my husband, Otley, said he wanted his.

'If we don't get it,' he said, 'they'll only go and give it to the Russians.' He couldn't fetch it himself as he was contemplating his navel so he sent me – I'm his errand boy.

They stamped the pension book with a capital 'B' for butter and handed it back with a silver brick-shaped object bearing the legend 'Produce of more than one country'. They must have a big melting pot under the station at Clapham Junction.

'It must be awful being on your own,' tutted the unlikely earth mother, her fat, bejewelled fingers still moving across the table, like sea-slugs on the ocean bed. My fingers itched to swat that do-gooding simper but her blue eyes, full of angst, sought out the next in line and I was jostled out into the cruel world.

'Look at him,' said an Irish leprechaun of a young blood getting into a flash car with a pound of butter. 'He won half a million on the pools last Christmas!'

'I expect it's for his mam,' explained a bedraggled Mohican, his red crest drooping like a sad cockatoo. 'She's got a bad leg.'

I put the loot into my plastic bag and hurried on, as Otley would be waiting for his Nescafé. The heavy gun-metal grey clouds burst; I lost my battle with the 'made in Taiwan' umbrella and a sudden rush of water sloshed off my oilskins and into my Wellington boots.

'What have you been doing all this time?' Otley wanted to know, as I squelched in. Without waiting for an answer, he snatched his pension book, stuck it to his forehead with a piece of Sellotape and went over to the mirror to see what a Common Market pauper looked like. He was a good-looking pauper with forest-green eyes and a fresh complexion – Dirty Denish, but with a disappearing hair-follicle situation.

'Do you think Interpol will want a photo?' he asked.

I put the treasure down on the kitchen table and we stood back to admire it; then, with a bellow of rage, Otley caught sight of the confession on its sleek, fat side.

'There'll be some German butter in that!' he exploded.

I had to agree and pointed out that we were all Europeans now.

'Well, I don't want it,' he said, out of the corner of his mouth, as if he didn't want it to hear. 'It's the becquerels.'

Since Chernobyl, he had been worried about the amount of radiation in our food chain and made frequent expeditions over the moors to see how many sheep had blue daubs on them. Never again would a lamb chop darken our doorstep, he kept saying.

'Never mind,' I said, and went to make some Nescafé.

The whole world knew, except me, he said, that West Germany had the highest number of becquerels, more even than Russia itself, as the wind had been blowing the wrong way. There was nothing for it but to go organic, send for a Geiger counter out of the *Exchange & Mart* and test everything before we ate it. What did I think about that, then? That Edward Heath had a lot to answer for – if it wasn't for him we would be eating New Zealand butter.

I hesitated for a moment.

'It's a good idea,' I said, with a carving knife pointed at my jugular. When he was agitated his eyes seemed to swivel in all directions, like a gecko. I mopped his brow and then gingerly took the knife out of his hand.

'I shall want that for the sandwiches,' I lied. For two pins I would have stuck it in his ribs, but war heroes have to be humoured. Arnhem did nothing for him but shake up his molecules, which had never settled down again; they rattled round inside his head like ball-bearings in a tin box. We were long married and what kept us together was a mystery, as we both fell in love with the frequency of the ginger tom in Bobbin Yard.

Perhaps it was the memory of that first kiss when we nearly choked, mouths full of gob-stoppers, on the old Victorian tramway going up to Shipley Glen. Or perhaps it was the fact that we had an awkward teenager, Mike, who showed every sign of going off the rails. We had to do our duty by him, hadn't we? We didn't want the magistrates asking 'Where are his mother and father?'

'Go and do your duty somewhere else!' Mike told us frequently.

He was at times, his loving papa declared, by way of being a git.

So we faced each other, all passion spent, under the glowering West Riding moors. Lightning-struck and storm-beset land; decaying mills silent as ships in the night, adrift and crewless like the *Mary Celeste*. Why worry about becquerels? Which is worse, dying of cancer in thirty years time, or getting run over by the ten fifty-five to Ilkley on a wet Monday morning?

'I'm not bothered about you lot,' Otley explained. 'It's the land; it'll be here when we've gone and they're buggering it up.'

The bold outcrops of millstone grit and the rushing waters of the high moors were what he liked. It was a man's world up there. I wanted the wooded valleys and the secret places where the purple bellflower grows.

A lump came into my throat at the thought of it being vaporized. We'd better get back to nature quick while it is still here! I could keep a nature diary – listen for the first cuckoo in spring; paint feathers and ladybirds everywhere and lie motionless for hours, waiting for something to come out of that hole in the banking at Ousel Beck. I would have to get a long frock and a big hat.

'We've got to look out for ourselves,' Otley was saying. 'They don't care; when they've made their money polluting here they'll be off to their chalets in Switzerland.'

My blood was boiling now. I moved over to the window and looked out at our Garden of Eden. The sun shone after the rain, stringing the trees with little diamonds; the cobbles glistened grey-green in the wet like frog spawn and a rainbow spanning the moor turned Allen's mill chimney into a stick of barley-sugar.

'Prevaricating mauleverers!' I shouted at the sky.

'. . . And it's no good talking to 'em,' he went on. 'They all suffer from plausible deniability like them at Irangate.'

He was winding me up again, talking me into his hare-brained schemes. Last year it was spying. Now he wants me to do-it-myself! Chernobyl, it seemed, had made the government look about as relevant as the waxworks Cabinet in Madame Tussaud's. He plunged the knife deep into the old pine table in his enthusiasm. I pulled it out, half expecting to see a message pinned to it. His back turned. A quick stab and it would be all over. He turned back again, this time with a sad look.

'Don't keep doing that,' I told him. 'It's losing its patina.'

I made some cheese-and-pickle sandwiches and then went to see what was on the goggle-box. It was 'talking heads', hands chopping the air in front of them with their thumbs up, live from Milton Keynes. Then there was a foreign film where the actors' mouths moved in between the words – Japanese, I think, as they kept bowing and walking on their knees and the women all had knitting needles in their heads.

'Aren't they polite,' I observed conversationally. 'Different from the men round these parts.'

'And different from the women,' he said. 'Wouldn't mind a nice little geisha girl to wash my feet.'

Wouldn't mind if you had, I said to myself, thinking of the smelly socks I found in the attic with the old *Private Eyes*. His socks had always been troublesome, coming out of the washing-machine felted up and in the wrong colour; and when the honeymoon was over and I was darning them under threat with big tears rolling down my cheeks, the whole family gathered round to gloat. With a bit of luck, when he went organic he'd go forth like Jesus, with bare feet and sandals.

'That would be nice,' I said.

He sat on in the best armchair like the Nizam of Hyderabad until it was time for *Their Lordships' House* at the witching hour and then he went to bed muttering something about pompous bloody creeps.

'Goodnight, love,' I called, thinking of the golden boy of Shipley Glen and hoping he was still there under the black storm clouds. If he wasn't, I would have to find another soulmate, still carrying out my official duties, of course, like royalty.

When the floorboards had stopped creaking upstairs, I tiptoed up past his room. If he heard me he would ask me to go and look at the Moon through his telescope. The house was as quiet as a ghost. No good peeping through Mike's keyhole to see what he was up to as he was at college. No scratchy old records playing in Myrtle's room; she had been whisked away by an affluent butcher into a world of patio doors and double glazing. Tom and Freda were still at the old mill keeping an eye on our summer visitors, rare as Dartford warblers. They'd had enough of Otley's spycatching last year and Freda wouldn't want to be parted from her split-level cooker to go organic. I was on my own.

I lingered at the casement before turning in. Bobbin Yard had taken on an eastern aspect since Sammy Chandra, confectioner and part-time astrologer, had moved in. A hawk-eyed Gujarati, forced to flee from Amin's Uganda in 1972, Sammy had decided to bring his gaudy sweetmeats to brighten up our grey northern clime. The mullioned windows, now trimmed with Christmas decorations, framed dishes of bright pink and yellow candy. Flocks of lively ladies would descend on him, like chattering birds of paradise, followed by children in assorted sizes from nought to ten like the King of Siam's. If only we could get them to join the amateur operatic society we could do *The King and I*. But not everybody was charmed.

'Tha wants thi passport to go theer,' Jimmy One Eye said, every time he came back from Bradford.

The new moon hung in the sky like a silver banana. Otley would be watching it through the second-hand telescope he got for his birthday. He wouldn't be able to see much. It's a shame.

'Did you hear that?' said Otley, the next morning, as we ate our boiled eggs and Marmite soldiers.

'No,' I said, stirring up the tea-bags.

'Unidentified flying object over Keighley last night, shook all the houses – no planes airborne at the time.'

'Why would they want to come here, then, when they've got all the universe to whizz about in?' I said, like Miss Marples.

'For the same reason the Arabs come here,' he said, 'they're after our water.'

So that's why it keeps disappearing! Ten months of steady drizzle and then, when the sun comes out, it's all gone. There was nothing for it, he said, but to start a UFO-watch; he had his telescope, hadn't he? He had read somewhere that the Russians had found a pile of radioactive dinosaur bones, which could mean that spacemen have been coming and going for yonks. All that stuff in the Bible as well – voices coming out of burning bushes; people coming down from the sky in a flash of light; people going back up in a puff of smoke. I knew it was God, of course, but Otley said it could have been a spaceman. We consulted Sammy Chandra and he said their gods were just the same, going up and down all the time.

'It is the main advantage of being a god,' he explained. 'They don't have escalators as they do on the Piccadilly Line.'

'All this thunder and lightning,' said Otley, 'it's got to be flying saucers sometimes – it's the law of averages.'

7

'Oh, Mr Craven, you are a very scientific fellow,' said Sammy. 'It is a disgrace that you have never won the Nobel prize.' Sammy folded up his charts, gave a stir to something smouldering in a brass bowl and escorted us to the door.

'My wife will show you how to make *rogan josh*,' he called after us.

At home, Otley fetched down the *Larousse Encyclopedia of Mythology* and examined it, while I scrubbed the kitchen floor.

'Red or yellow, black or white, they all come down in a flash of light.' For a minute I thought he was going to do a song and dance like Fred Astaire, but he had only slipped on the soap, coming to show me a picture. It was a square man with a round head cut out of a lump of stone in Mexico.

'There's one here with a space helmet on,' he said.

I could well believe that he had come out of a flying saucer as he was not at all like the gentle Jesus meek and mild on the wall at the Christian Endeavour. And all those people who say they've seen flying saucers. They're not all drunken sots coming back from the office party; some of them are quite respectable.

'Pillars of society,' said Otley, 'airline pilots, highway patrolmen, responsible citizens.' He puffed himself up like an amorous bull-frog.

'But it's no good being a responsible washerwoman and seeing a flying saucer,' he said, looking at me, 'because nobody will believe you.'

Not being of a scientific turn of mind, I said I didn't want to see flying saucers anyway. Little green men so soon after Chernobyl would be more than I could cope with. And us a nuclear-free zone as well! Keighley had 780 becquerels per litre of rainwater after Chernobyl, nearly 8,000 times the normal. Our councillors complained to the Soviet Peace Delegation, who were in Shipley at the time.

'I thought there was something funny about that rain,' Otley said. 'It stung like a bee and I had red spots on my hands with it.'

Otley and I had some fast food – jam and bread and a drink of milk. Our old family doctor, a canny Scot, always told mother that brown bread and jam and a glass of milk was a meal fit for a king. That suits me.

'You'll have to start cooking macrobiotic like the Third World,' said Otley, licking his milk moustache off. 'Bamboo shoots in a wok.'

'But I haven't got a wok,' I protested.

'Then bloody well get one,' he said.

I warned him last year after the spycatching episode that if he didn't mend his ways I was going to apply for sheltered accommodation. People come and sing for you; they take you shopping in a minibus and when you die, you just press a buzzer. When I fell in love and got married I didn't expect all this aggravation. We used to sing a song in the Mixed Infants about a fine lady running off with the gypsies:

> 'She-he pluck-ed off her-er high-heeled shoo-oo-s
> a-made of Span-i-sh leather-O,
> And she laid down her-er si-hilken gown
> For to go with the raggle-taggle gypsies-O'.

How I envied that great lady, throwing off the shackles of wealth to go free as a bird with her bold gypsy boy. The rolling road, a bed under the stars, the harvest moon above like a ripe Cheshire cheese. They didn't tell you what happened next, when she had to go selling clothes-pegs and then come back and clean that dirty, greasy, black iron pot full of rabbits they hang over the fire. Then Granny went and taught us another song to sing when we were skipping:

> 'My mother said I never should
> Play with the gypsies in the wood.'

But we didn't know who to believe; one of them was lying.

'Do your own macrobiotic cooking,' I said, on reflection.

'What for?' He seemed quite put out.

'You'll have to do it when I'm dead, won't you?'

'No, I won't, I'll go round the chip shop.' He smirked.

'Well, go round the chip shop now, then,' I said recklessly.

His eyes started to swivel and I put the bread knife away quick. He was really quite handsome, on the rampage. Like Ernest Hemingway at a bull fight; but he needed watching at full moon. He chased me round the kitchen and then, when he caught me, said he had to go and write some letters. Would I mind popping up to High Riding where they do alternative living weeks and see if they have any vacancies for us? Before we mangle our own garden we can practise on somebody else's. I thought, run your own flamin' errands. Who do you think you are – Sultan of bloody Zanzibar? But it was a nice day and I wanted to be in my Edwardian Lady mood. I could wander up there with my nature diary.

'Why, of course,' I said graciously, 'I'd be delighted.'

'Are you all right?' he asked.

'Capital, my dear fellow. How civilized of you to inquire.'

'Have you got a bloke up there or something?' he wanted to know.

'An admirer?' I said, with a tinkling laugh, like a silver bell, 'I think not.'

'No, I mean somebody you're having it off with,' he said.

'Really! Such vulgarisms! I must insist you stop seeing that common gel behind the bar at the Rose and Crown.'

'Seriously, have you got a bloke?' he persisted.

'Not yet, my dear Crispin – not yet,' I said, sweeping out of the room.

THE NEXT MORNING I got all my nature diary stuff ready in the attic: a long skirt and a frilly blouse; pencils and paint brushes in a jam jar; a sketching pad from Woolworths; Mike's old school ruler and a rubber that looks like a bar of chocolate; an old toothbrush that makes it look as if it's raining in the painting and twelve boxes of water colours made in Shanghai.

I could write my notes outside sitting under a tree in the garden and paint my feathers and ladybirds in the attic; there's a great demand for nature diaries these days and in any case if nobody wants it in the end, it will do for posterity.

I could just about squeeze into the skirt, which was a grey bombazine one out of Granny Hawkweed's dead drawer; the blouse was faded linen with pink ribbons threaded down the front and it went nicely with the straw hat I had brought back from Blackpool, tied on with a chiffon scarf. I might have been all right for the London to Brighton Old Crocks' race. I certainly was not fit for any other kind of race, unless it was in the water when my spare tyre would hold me up a treat. Confronting myself in the mirror is a bit of an ordeal. Middle-aged spread, eyes the colour of bluebells fading in the sun and hair like dried-up corn stalks left over from the harvest. I still think of myself as the golden-haired sprite of yester-year, the Princess Diana of Quarry Bottoms. I do try. I do everything Barbara Cartland tells you to but only succeed in looking like a Cabbage Patch doll.

I rushed down into the kitchen garden where nobody could see me, eager to start my journal.

3 July 2 AC (After Chernobyl)
Crispin and I back from our constitutional through the sunny meadows. The air heavy with the scent of meadow-sweet and honeysuckle. With a little cry I came upon a clump of monkey flowers, their merry, freckled faces beaming at us like a lot of Fergies. Crispin gallantly risked drowning to bring me back a nosegay. Dear man! How I never cease to bless the day the angels sent him to me!
We tarried a while to observe a family of ducks darting among the reeds (what comical chaps they are!) and I endeavoured to capture their antics in my sketchbook while Crispin partook of seven coconut kisses. Inspired to compose, I penned a few modest words:

> Look out! little mallard,
> You'll be hitting the bollard.

We meandered back to our little love-nest in the dell, pausing only to listen to the hum of the countryside all rampant in the warmth of the summer sun. A tear came into my eye and Crispin gave my hand a squeeze. Dear Crispin!

'What the bloody hell are you doing? Skivin' again?' Otley

appeared from nowhere like the demon king in a panto-
mime. He seemed to be upset about something and held out
a crumpled shirt towards me.

'When are you going to sew the bloody buttons on this
shirt?'

'In a minute,' I said, with great presence of mind. 'I'm
just finishing this – it's my nature diary.'

'Never mind nature diary,' he said, snatching it out of
my hand. 'I haven't had my breakfast yet!'

'Give me it back!' I screamed, as we struggled for possession. 'I'll kill you if you don't give me it back!'

'What do you want to do a nature diary for?' he asked, as
we grappled with the diary down the garden path. 'You
had one from the library last year, didn't you? Won't be as
good as that.'

'It's for posterity,' I sobbed.

'He won't want it,' he said. 'It's a waste of time.'

After we had exhausted ourselves, we negotiated a deal.
He would let me carry on with my diary if I kept his socks
and shirts in working order. Anything for a quiet life,
although socks and shirts are the two things I hate most in
life. Why didn't I marry an intellectual, instead of a war
hero? Macho-men are so tiring. That's why I've never been
to Spain – all that stamping and flaring nostrils; it's enough
to give you a splitting headache.

'I thought you were going up to High Riding today?'
Otley said as I sewed on the last button. He hadn't time to
go himself as he had to go and get some money out of the
Bradford & Bingley and send for a Geiger counter from
Exchange & Mart, ready for our alternative living.

'You can observe some wildlife on the way,' he said.

I took off my Edwardian lady outfit and changed into
jeans and a cotton top, as I didn't want to frighten the
horses going up to High Riding. The Miss Brooks, Thelma
and Sylvie, were distant cousins of Otley but we hadn't seen

them since Granny Hawkweed's funeral. The house, Victorian Gothic, was falling down around them, and the garden a wilderness. Still, it would be a pleasant walk.

'And don't forget to get a wok down the market,' Otley called after me.

Get your own bloody wok, I thought to myself, as I shut the door.

'All right,' I shouted.

I followed the beck along the valley bottom where it was lined with Himalayan balsam and Japanese knotweed. How they got here and why they decided to stay is one of life's unsolved mysteries, like when you bake a custard pie and the crust comes out on top.

Past Allen's mill lurking in the long grass, its chimney rising from a sea of rosebay willowherb like the neck of the Loch Ness monster. Up to the moor where every step sends a cloud of moths and butterflies out of the heather, and on to where you know the trees are hiding a pile of ivy-covered bricks that calls itself a house.

I fought my way through nettles and brambles to the lion's head brass knocker on the front door. The sound of it echoed inside like the crack of doom. The door creaked open slowly and a pair of fluttering hands appeared round it. That would be cousin Sylvie. Cousin Thelma would be out on the moors; she had plundered the world in her younger days collecting butterflies and was often to be seen striding out with a knapsack and butterfly net, for a day in the wild. Cousin Sylvie was a fey, sensitive creature who liked to wander barefoot in the moonlight and do Grecian dancing in filmy draperies. One day, she thought, her prince would come.

There was no love lost between them and it was said that Thelma would like to pin Sylvie to a piece of cardboard and keep her in the drawer with the other pathetic little bodies. But blood is thicker than paper and we all stick together, no matter how much we hate each other.

'It's May,' I said. 'Otley's wife.'

'Oo!' she squealed, 'Let's have a cup of tea.'

I followed the draperies into the parlour, where Sylvie plugged in a teasmaid which poured out some bakelite tea. Yellow-dyed curls escaped from pink ribbon bows and her rouged face dimpled, making her look like an elderly Shirley Temple going into a dance. Sylvie would exchange High Riding for 'The Good Ship Lollipop' any day of the week.

'We're thinking of doing alternative living for a week or so,' I told her. 'It'll be a change, anyway, from *Dallas* and *Coronation Street*.'

'Thelma does the booking,' she said, fluttering over to the window in an aura of sweet-pea-coloured chiffon. Her violet-blue eyes anxiously watched the driveway for a sign of life.

'We just want to try it,' I said. 'See what it's like first.'

She made a quick movement backwards like a startled willow warbler. 'You never invited us to the wedding,' she said, 'and it was disgusting what they did at the funeral.'

At every wedding and funeral somebody went home offended, so I didn't bother to ask which ones. It could be any one of a dozen or more.

'I'm sorry,' I lied.

'And Thelma's never got over Otley pouring his rhubarb and custard into her best Sunday hat.'

'He was naughty, wasn't he?' I said sympathetically.

'And that day on the Whitsuntide Walk, when he stuck a squashed beetle inside my currant bun.' She shuddered at the memory of it.

'I know,' I said.

'And at the Sunday Sing when he pushed me in a cow-clap with my new white silk frock on and my gold bangle.'

'He was a real Dennis the Menace,' I said light-heartedly.

'We like to be quiet at night,' she went on. 'We like a bit

of culture – Radio Three an' that – we don't want riff-raff lowering the tone.'

'Oh! he'll be UFO-watching at night,' I said. 'You won't know he's here.'

'Has he given up spying, then?' She gave a twirl and then ran on tiptoe to the opposite window like a fleeing nymph.

'Chernobyl's made him more socially aware,' I said, trying to sound as if I knew what I was talking about.

'More socially aware than Shirley Williams?' She inquired.

'About the same,' I said, with a wild guess. She fled to the radio and put some mood music on, then settled gracefully on the sofa with her arms waving like madonna lilies in the evening breeze.

'I'm glad Thelma's gone out,' she said dreamily. 'I can put what I like on – she has all that Big Daddy stuff on, Beethoven an' that. Ugh! I can't stand it.'

'It's not bad for somebody who's deaf,' I said.

'Hope she sticks in a bog and doesn't come back, then I can have some Paraguayan harp music.'

The front door creaked open followed by firm footsteps, and a fine figure of a woman joined us in the parlour. A relic of the Raj, skin the colour and texture of coconut matting and with the fearsome aspect of a deranged dacoit, Thelma hung her butterfly net and squashed hat on the back of a chair and switched off the radio.

'I'm not listening to that maungy drivel,' she said. 'Get off out and get some exercise. Mooching about all day long – no wonder you can't sleep at night and have to go off with the hobgoblins.'

'You were out,' said Sylvie, 'and I was all alone.'

'Well I'm in now, aren't I?' Thelma said, her black eyes flashing.

'Did you catch anything?' Sylvie wanted to know.

'Only a few miserable, poxy little moths; I'll feed 'em to

the Venus Flytrap. What's this?' she inquired as if I were a specimen.

'It's me,' I said. 'I've come to book an alternative-living week.'

'You can have the garden cottage; no room in the house, we've got some morris dancers coming next week.' She took off her safari jacket and a moth flew out. 'But don't expect any room service.'

'Oh! we don't,' I said. 'We want to practise doing-it-our-selves.'

Thelma strode over to the radio and twiddled the knobs until she found something to her liking: trumpets, drums and crashing cymbals. She had worn three husbands out while Sylvie waited for Prince Charming.

'I'll be off now, then. See you on Saturday,' I said, waving and inclining my head like the Queen Mother does on her birthday. Sylvie followed me to the door and clung to it like a wet butterfly waiting for its wings to dry out.

'I told you, didn't I? She always does it. I can't stand it! Crash, bang, wallop; boom bang-a-bang; oompah, oompah, stick it up your jumper; I'll brain her with it one of these days.' Her eyes had a wild look.

'Why don't you buy another one?' I suggested.

''Cos it's mine; Mummy gave me it when the moonflowers were out; it's got magic in it.' Her haunted eyes knew something I didn't.

'They're cheap enough in Woolworths,' I couldn't help saying.

'I don't want a nasty little Hong Kong one; why doesn't she buy one? *That's* mine.' Her wings were dry now and she was ready to flutter off and be caught in Thelma's net.

'See you Saturday, then,' I called, as I picked my way down the weed-strewn flags. Now I had to go and get a wok.

*

'A what?' said Alf Pickersgill on the market stall, his brown eyes all agog.

'It's what the Chinese cook vegetables in,' I explained.

'Never 'eard of it. Thought they ate birds' nests, anyway.'

'An' sea-slugs,' said his wife, coming up from under the counter. 'They gave the Queen sea-slugs when she was in China.'

I could have got an aluminium one but you can get senile decay eating off aluminium, I read somewhere; and when posh people get it they call it a fancy name, Alzheimer's disease, or something. Same sort of thing as when royalty go mad and they call it porphyria. I found the real thing in 'Star of the East Emporium', with an instruction book, standing ring, steamer rack, draining and tempura rack, ladle, spatula, rice paddle, a pair of serving chopsticks, ten pairs of chopsticks to eat with and a hundred skewers. So we should be all right. And if it rains I can always turn it upside down and put it on my head.

'Oh! Mrs Craven, what you got there?' Sammy Chandra shook his head sadly. 'That's no bloody good; you cook Indian like I say.'

'We're just trying it out,' I said. 'Going organic for a week.'

'Only rabid dogs go organic; my wife will show you how to make a damn good curry.' He was putting boxes of brightly coloured sweetmeats into the back of his tinsel-trimmed Fiesta. His keen dark eyes scanned the horizon for prospective customers. 'You want to buy some jaggery?'

'I'm on a diet,' I told him, pointing to my middle-aged spread.

'Too much bloody Yorkshire pudding.' He got into the car and leaned out of the window. 'There is a commotion in your stars. Take great care: Saturn, Uranus, Mars and Pluto in opposition to your ruling planet Venus – many trouble.'

'There always is.' I laughed. 'I'm used to it by now.'

Otley was waiting for some fast food so I practised with the wok. It took only ten minutes to cook it but an hour to get it ready. Slivers of carrots, onions, peppers, leeks, mushrooms, garlic, white wine and soy sauce, with ginger and beansprouts tossed in nonchalantly at the last minute, fried in sesame oil – nothing so common as margarine.

'Is that it?' said Otley, looking crestfallen.

'I'd forgotten, it's got to be served on brown rice,' I said. 'Wait a minute while I put it on.'

'How long will it take?' he asked anxiously.

'About forty minutes,' I said. 'It takes longer than white.'

'Don't bother,' he said. 'I'll make a sandwich.'

We had a struggle getting it all between two slices of bread and the floor was littered with beansprouts. It tasted a bit like shredded parsnips dipped in gripe-water, with a dash of Angostura Bitters.

'If that's what they eat no wonder they all want to come over here,' Otley said. 'Get some proper food for a change.'

'It's very healthy,' I said, looking at the recipe book. 'I'll try a different one next time.'

'There's no cats in there, is there?' he asked suspiciously.

'It's mostly vegetarian.' As I flicked through the pages my heart sank into my boots. Water-lilies made out of tomatoes; rosettes made out of spring onions; dinky little parcels of rice wrapped in seaweed; pancakes you can see through and prawns balancing on the end of a stick. No wonder those poor old Chinese women you see on Channel Four are all skin and bone – they never get time to eat.

'We can use the wok for making chips in,' I said, getting up to go. 'I'm off to paint some ladybirds.'

'Have you booked us in at High Riding?' Otley asked, patting his hair down and smoothing his tie as if he were going to a dance.

'Just for a week,' I said, 'from next Saturday.'

'Better start packing, then, never mind ladybirds.'

Thump! I thought to myself, as I ran upstairs. I had to get myself in the mood so I changed into my costume again and settled down to paint. I had twelve boxes of Chinese watercolours with twenty tubes in each box, enough to make a million ladybirds if I wanted. I smiled at the prospect and set to work. After that I painted Crispin's hand holding out a nosegay, and a mallard feeding among the reeds – that was easy, I just did a triangle with feathers on. I put a blob of blue paint and scrabbled it with the toothbrush to make it look like water and I painted a big sun like the Japanese flag up in the corner. That would be enough for today. I was just rinsing the brushes out when Otley banged on the door.

'I can't find my grey shirt. Where've you put it?' he called.

'It's having the buttons sewn on,' I shouted back.

'Who's sewing 'em on – the fairies?' he jeered.

'I'll be down in a minute,' I said, 'when I've tidied up.'

'What you up to in there, writing love letters?'

'My secret admirer, remember?' I laughed gaily.

'Open this door or I'll break it down,' he demanded.

'Why don't you go fishing or something – I'm doing my diary,' I said.

'I'm going round the pub when I find my shirt.' He seemed to be scraping in the keyhole with a metal object and suddenly the door swung open and he stumbled in with a wire coat-hanger in his hand.

'You're not supposed to do that until you've sewn my buttons on.' He picked up my diary, read it quickly and then waved it in front of my face. 'Who's this bloody Crispin, then?' He gobbled like a mad turkey.

'Nobody, I'm making it up,' I said, grabbing it back.

'It's that bloke up at High Riding, isn't it?'

'There's nobody up there, only your cousins, and they're as mad as hatters,' I said, wishing I hadn't married into a lunatic asylum.

'I'll bet,' he said. 'Why have you got to make a bloke up for your diary? Why can't you put me in it?'

'I wanted somebody romantic and poetic – that's all. Somebody a bit effeminate; you're so masterful and rugged,' I lied.

'You're a crafty little devil,' he said, narrowing his eyes. The evening sun glinted into them, lighting them up like cats' eyes in the road. I moved the paper-knife out of his way.

'I have to pretend,' I explained. 'Nobody wants to read about *us*; I have to make out I'm married to the curate and we've got a wood-burning stove and a bain-marie.'

'Just don't forget my shirts, that's all; we're going on a UFO-watch tonight – I shall want all my buttons on as it might turn chilly.'

Please God, I prayed, as I ran down the stairs, let him be kidnapped by a flying saucer and put into orbit round Jupiter or somewhere.

THE NEXT MORNING a Geiger counter arrived by post and Otley examined it with dismay, knee-deep in packings and instruction leaflets. It was like a malformed toaster with a carrying handle and what looked like a cosh on the end of an elephant's trunk.

'It's got no becquerels,' said Otley, crestfallen.

'It must have,' I said, picking up a leaflet then dropping it when I caught a glimpse of '0.05 to 75μSv/h (0.005 to 7.5mr/h)'.

'It's only got milliSieverts,' he said in disgust.

'What are they?' I asked.

'I don't know,' he said testily.

'Well – as long as it clicks,' I said soothingly, 'take no notice of 'em.'

He plugged it in near the television and it clicked away like mad.

'It goes on batteries as well,' he said, as he uncoupled it, 'so I can take it up on the moors.'

'You can go with old Inky Popplewell when he exercises

the dog,' I said, gathering up the debris to put in the litter-bin.

'What's this?' Otley said, opening a letter which we had overlooked in our excitement at getting the Geiger counter. It was a begging letter from Mike at the Ridings Polytechnic, where he was meant to be studying psychology and sociology. Could we send him £10 and would we mind letting him and his friends use the house for a few weeks, as they'd formed a new pop group and they had nowhere to practise for the college rag week? We could go to Benidorm on a SAGA holiday, couldn't we? The longer we stayed, the cheaper it would be, he said. It would be like a second honeymoon and we wouldn't want to come back here.

'I'll murder him,' Otley raged. 'Impudent young git!'

'We can stay up at High Ridings longer,' I suggested. 'A week's not really long enough for doing-it-yourself.' It would keep them out of each other's way for two months and as far as I was concerned prolonged wokking, tedious though it may be, was preferable to visiting the local nick with food parcels for the rest of my life. Forming groups seemed to be as full of hazards as a 'Spot the Ball' competition and Mike's continually changed its shape – forming and reforming, dividing, subdividing and coming together again with the skill of an amoeba. They needed a bit of help. Luckily it occurred to Otley that if this group was a success and they got on *Top of the Pops* it would mean them going on a world tour – they could have the house after all.

'But I'm not going to Benidorm. Bloody cheek!' he said.

There was a documentary on the box that night about the Seychelles being the original Garden of Eden because big nuts grow there in the shape of a woman's behind. Well, there's nothing like that up at High Riding and I hoped that Otley wouldn't be too disappointed. There was always Bella at the Rose & Crown if he got fed up with doing it himself. I knew when he was going to see her because he left his shirt open to show his hairy chest and wore his gold medallion round his neck like Tom Jones. It gave me the chance to have a quiet cuppa and get on with my diary.

4 July 2 AC

Evening falls and My Lady Moon bathes all in her gentle light. A skein of wild geese honk a greeting to me as they skim the silver lake on their way to roost. I return their honk. Dear feathered ones! The jewelled dragonfly darts no longer in the sedge. The water-lily, Lady of the Lake, secretly dips her face into the cool depths for her nightly booze. My beloved Crispin, ever mindful of the needs of others, has taken a sustaining broth to a sick cottager in a nearby hamlet and will not fail to gather kindling on his return. I shall keep his repast waiting in the bain-marie. It is nought but tripe and onions. Honest Crispin! Honk!

Now I'd have to paint some wild geese in flight; the ducks on the wall that Mike won on the coconut shy would be a good stand-in; Willy Lott's 'Cottage' on the kitchen wall that we got down the market for seventy-five pence could go in, with Crispin's hand holding out a bowl of soup to an old man dressed like Wee Willie Winkie, the church bells ringing up in the clouds and a dragonfly riding on the clappers. Where was I going to get a dragonfly at this time of night? I'd have to wait until tomorrow and see if Thelma had one in the drawer.

We had decided to go up to High Riding on the Sunday as Saturday was going to be a busy day for the Miss Brooks, with the Ruddlestones morris men arriving early and wanting 'seeing to', as Thelma put it, so it gave me a chance to do some last-minute sorting out. We were taking as little as possible and would wash our things out in the beck. No detergents to pollute the land and no aerosols to make holes in the ozone layer. No good trying to grow anything in that short space of time, so we were taking a sack of rice and a hundredweight of carrots, onions and potatoes, and we would gather the wild harvest of the fields and hedgerows and go on fungus forays in dawn's early light.

I went upstairs to hide Otley's shirts and socks that wanted mending, and suddenly the room was flooded with light: red, then green, red again and then a bluish white. I rushed to the window to see what it was, thinking it might be the street lamp shining on Sammy Chandra's Christmas decorations. But there was something hovering above the houses. A light blinked on and off in patterns, like the Blackpool illuminations, and another orange ball of light came rolling over the moors and seemed to vanish into it. There was a humming noise like a swarm of giant bees and the house vibrated as the thing shot upwards into the sky. In no time at all it was just a speck in the distance, one of a myriad stars. I was still shaking as I ran downstairs and out into the street. Otley met me, white as a ghost himself and out of breath from a long run down from the moor, his telescope and Geiger counter forgotten inside his rucksack.

'Did you see it?' he asked, when he'd got his breath back.

'I did,' I told him, adding some dramatic highlights. 'It looked in at me through the bedroom window!'

'It chased us across the moors in Percy Dredger's old banger,' he went on. 'We couldn't shake it off.'

He'd been to the Rose & Crown first for a little aperitif, he said, then they'd gone UFO-watching, just him and Percy, up by the tarn. They saw this light on the water and stopped to see what it was. Then it was in front of them on the road, blocking the way down to Low Riding. They had to turn round and take the Colne road to get away but it hung on their tail. They thought they'd dodged it when they made a U-turn at Laneshaw Bridge, but it was there in front of them. They went hell for leather through Stanbury and over Lower Laithe reservoir where it seemed to stop to look at the water and they thought they'd given it the slip, but when they got as far as Allen's mill where you turn up towards High Riding, it was there waiting for them on the Halifax Road.

'Well, you went looking for UFOs, didn't you?' I said.

'Yes, but *you* didn't,' he replied sharply.

We heard later that Mrs Broadhead up at Four Winds Farm saw a silver man about seven feet tall poking a dead sheep with a stick. He vanished into thin air when she asked him what he was up to. He had pointed ears and pink eyes that slanted up with no lids. Otley found this encouraging and couldn't wait for the next UFO-watch.

'They're trying to tell us something,' he said, loading the potatoes into the back of the car. 'Have you mended my green striped shirt?' I had only packed denims and T-shirts. You can't go native in smart, natty gents' suiting. It doesn't go with woks.

'I couldn't find it,' I lied.

For once he didn't seem to care. His eyes had a new sparkle, his step, a new bounce. We rattled our way up to High Riding like an old tinker's cart, the front seat piled up with cooking pots and plastic bags full of old clothes. I sat in the back with the potatoes and a sack of rice on my knee.

It was a warm sunny day, drowsy with bees, and we stopped on Penistone Way to take in the views. The blue water of Lower Laithe set like a sapphire in the gold-tipped meadows; the high moors, a rolling purple sea and the bright splash of green that was the wooded river valley. There was no need to say anything. If the angels flung us out of heaven on to the heath below we would lie sobbing for joy like Cathy Earnshaw. Always assuming that we got to heaven in the first place. There's an old story of an ambitious tyke who knocked on the pearly gates to see what would happen. They swung open and out came St Peter, who shook his head angrily.

'You can't come in,' he said. 'We're not making Yorkshire Pudding for one.'

As we turned into the drive at High Riding there was a sound of clashing sticks and jingle bells and a leaping morris man chased after a blown-up bladder that went this way and that, like one of those crazy balls you buy at the seaside. We screeched to a halt to avoid them and a flowered head appeared at the window.

'I'm sorry,' he said, 'you don't know what it's going to do next.'

'Do you know you just missed being killed?' Otley said.

'I just missed being killed last week as well,' the flowered one said, with a wink in my direction. He was slender and fair, and my face reddened under the saucy looks. His designer stubble came nearer and I saw that if he was a faun he was an ageing one. Not that it mattered to me, anyway. Otley started up the engine and we shot forward.

'Well, watch it,' he warned. 'Third time pays for all.'

The old cottage was clean and dry but Spartan. White-washed walls, stone-flagged kitchen with brodded rugs, stone sink with a cold water tap and a tin bath hanging on the wall. I picked up a besom, the sort that witches fly about on, and flicked some dead leaves out into the garden. This was going to be fun, like playing at Hansel and Gretel.

Otley carried a portable television into the sitting-room and put it on a three-legged spindle table opposite the put-u-up.

'That's cheating,' I said. 'The Third World don't have televisions in their mud huts.'

'Well, you don't think I'm going to sit staring at you all night, do you?' he said, looking at the Radio Times. 'No need to go to extremes.'

After we had unpacked, we went to see the wilderness – Thelma's butterfly garden. Nettles, thistles, ragworts, Jack-go-to-bed-at-noon; Billy Buttons, codlins-and-cream, Queen

27

Anne's lace, creeping-jenny, fat hen, Good King Henry, lords and ladies, stinking iris, ragged robin and Sylvie's moon flowers strangling everything in sight – bindweed some call it – it would be a good corner for doing my diary.

'Have you sewn my buttons on yet?' Otley said, breaking the spell.

'Bast and blugger your buddy bluttons!' I stormed, incoherent in my fury, scattering all in my path as I rushed into the kitchen.

'Aren't you making any dinner?' enquired Otley in hurt tones.

We had cheese-and-pickle sandwiches, and plugged the electric jug in to make some tea. This was make or break time. The next few weeks would decide for me whether to apply for sheltered accommodation or not. The British Legion was building some down in Dingle Bottoms; as an ex-servicewoman myself I might stand a chance. They have Bingo every night and a barbecue on the sands at Dunkirk every summer.

'Don't get upset,' Otley said, pouring me out another mug of tea. 'I don't like to see you upset.'

'You don't care about me,' I said sulkily.

'Yes I do,' he said.

'No you don't.' I pouted like Brigitte Bardot.

'All right, then, I don't,' he said, combing his hair and changing into his best shirt and trousers. He'd sneaked them in, after all.

'Where are you going to?' I asked, sniffing into my handkerchief.

'I'm just off for a little aperitif,' he said.

'Mind how you go,' I called after him.

It was a game we played. There were times when I prayed he would fall down a disused mine shaft on his way back. I expect I would miss him if he did, just as I missed the old wardrobe that fell on top of you every time you opened the door.

I finished unpacking, dragged the potatoes into an alcove and then stood the sack of rice by the side of it. They looked like Darby and Joan. What a gay day! Then I took my things up into the bedroom. Slanting ceiling; faded carpet; brass bed with a patchwork quilt; washstand with cracked jug and bowl; dead wasp in the soap-dish; lattice window holding on for dear life. Poor, but honest. It could have been worse. Otley would be sleeping downstairs on the put-u-up. We liked separate rooms. At first I felt guilty about it, but then I thought, what's good enough for the Queen and Prince Philip is good enough for me. And there was no telephone. If you wanted anybody to know anything you would have to send a messenger. Later I went to the big house.

From the outside, High Riding itself looks a bit like something out of a Hammer horror film – all weird chimneys and spooky corners. Inside wasn't too bad: lots of squashy, chintz-covered armchairs and eccentric windows with sudden views of the moors. A little Edwardian conservatory with rampaging Swiss cheese plants, parlour palms and potted begonias faced south over the valley, furnished with a white, plastic table and chairs from Woolworths.

'Very Noël Coward, isn't it?' The voice came out of the jungle.

Who could it be? A soberly clad figure emerged from behind a clump of ferns and for a minute I didn't realize who it was.

'I'm sorry,' I said, 'I didn't recognize you with your clothes on.' All those music-hall jokes were true then. People did say things like that. He said he was Jeff Ashley from Catstone Clough.

'What are you here for?' he asked, as if it were Wormwood Scrubs.

'Seeing how little we can live on; back-to-nature stuff,' I said.

'And us,' he said. 'We need to get some weight off; this

morris dancing gives you beer bellies, calling in at every pub.'

'It's not self-sufficiency we're doing,' I hastened to add. 'We don't want to get involved in pig-killing and hanging sausages up.'

'I know,' he said with feeling.

'We're not into keeping sheep and goats either,' I explained. 'It's too much like being a registered childminder.'

'And they get things like scrapie and cloudburst,' he sympathized, examining a jasmine flower. 'Hardly worth the bother.'

'Chickens get fowlpest,' I said, trying to sound intelligent.

'We've brought some Goldenlay eggs from the Co-op,' he said.

By now we were getting to know each other. He was an unemployed steelworker from Sheffield; all the knives and forks come from Taiwan, these days. He'd bought a cottage with his redundancy money and was interested in reviving all the old English customs, like bundling, gurning, dwyle-flonking and fertility rites. There was a boulder on Rombald's Moor with a hole in it, he said, and if you could squeeze through it that meant you would meet your true-love at midnight and have triplets within a year.

'What, at my age?' I laughed, thinking only of the last bit.

'It's never too late to meet your true-love,' he assured me. 'My Great Aunt Zoe, who used to be on the stage, got married at ninety and wrote a book on her honeymoon called *Up the Amazon with a Gaiety Girl*; her poor husband died of yellow fever and she came back with a Bolivian tin-miner.'

'There's hope for me yet,' I knew I was expected to say.

We wandered out into the evening air, through the overgrown garden with brambles snatching at our arms and legs. There was a dreamlike quality about it, like

Sleeping Beauty's garden, and Jeff was a pleasant companion. I could enjoy him without having to mend his smelly socks at the end of it. I looked down at his feet. They were as naked as the day he was born! And sandalled! My dreamboat! My ideal man! My soulmate!

'Was that your old man in the car?' he wanted to know.

'Yes.' I held my breath; was he jealous?

'We could do with another morris man,' he said.

I said I'd tell him and asked if a morris woman would do instead. No, certainly not. The lads wouldn't stand for it. It was a tradition that morris dancers had to be men and they didn't want girls hanging round them in pubs.

'I'm hardly a girl,' I pointed out.

'You were once,' he said accusingly.

I couldn't deny it so I tried another tack.

'I'll report you to the Race Relations Board,' I said wildly.

'Don't you mean the Equal Opportunities Commission?' he said.

'That as well,' I said, 'and the European Court of Human Rights.'

If all else failed, I could write to the Queen. I was already composing a letter in my mind; as an honorary man herself she would understand.

May it please Your Majesty, in your capacity as Duke of Lancaster, to intervene in the dispute between I, May Craven, an Ancient Briton, and the Ruddlestones morris men who will not admit me to their company as a morris man. Hoping this finds you as it leaves me at present.

'Don't forget to mention it to him, anyway,' Jeff reminded me. I found myself in the wilderness and him bounding away like a springbok.

'Was that that bloody Crispin?' asked Otley who was

back early from the Rose & Crown. Bella had gone to Majorca on a bucket-shop ticket out of the Sunday papers and he was at a loose end.

'It was one of the morris dancers,' I told him. 'The one you nearly ran over; he said would you like to join 'em?'

'What me?' he said. 'Capering about with bells and a funny hat on!'

'You always wore funny hats at Blackpool,' I reminded him.

'That's different,' he said. 'It's the seaside.'

We watched some 'talking heads' on the box with their thumbs up; an Indian extravaganza where the lovers look into each other's eyes for ten minutes and run in and out of the trees, and then the dancing girls come on, stirring up a cloud of dust like a twister in the Arizona desert. Then there was a suburban situation-comedy where Mummy keeps saying, 'Dinner's in the oven, darling. I'm just off to the pottery class'; but when John Wayne came on in *True Grit* for the umptieth time, we threw in the towel.

'Might as well be dead,' said Otley, switching off the set.

'You speak for yourself,' I muttered, as I went to do the washing-up.

'What did you say?' he wanted to know.

'I said, this looks like Delft,' I lied, holding up a blue-and-white plate for his inspection.

'I THINK I'LL go over and see if Thelma's got any dragonflies,' I said, dusting down my best jeans and patting my hair into place.

'What d'you want dragonflies for?' asked Otley.

'For my nature diary,' I said. 'They're too fast to paint on the wing, not suitable material for field study.'

I hoped I was impressing him with my scientific knowledge and that he would henceforth take my diary seriously, but it was not to be.

'Get a daddy-long-legs and pull the legs off,' he suggested.

There was no doubt he had a cruel streak. He could have been a surgeon instead of a madman. He might as well wander over there with me, he said. Keep the old girls company. Brighten up their lives, poor old souls. It must be lonely living up here, especially in the wintertime. All right for Emily Brontë and that lot, but we can't all write poetry.

'The moor was her inspiration,' I protested.

'Come off it,' he said. 'She had a bloke somewhere; all them love poems – where d'you think they came from?'

33

'She communed with nature,' I said angrily. 'It was a mystic love, she had no need of anything else, just the wind in the heather and the twinkling firmament.'

'Get away with you,' he jeered. 'She was having it off with the curate.'

Otley was already arrayed in his Sunday best anyway and he thought it would be a pity to waste it on me. He took off his gold medallion, buttoned up his green poplin shirt and put on his green silk tie. Now he looked like a grasshopper going to the Butterfly Ball. He turned to examine me as we closed the door and stepped out on to the garden path. Did I look all right? I wondered.

'Know what you look like in jeans and that floppy yellow top?'

'No, what?' I asked eagerly.

'You look like an aubergine with Birds custard sloshed over it.'

'Oh!' I said, 'never mind.'

Sylvie let us in and fluttered down the hall into the sitting-room, where Thelma was entertaining the morris men with tales of how she had been captured by bandits while hunting the Acraea Violae in Ceylon. Her lean, vibrant body turned this way and that acting it all out as if in a game of charades.

'And how did you escape?' somebody asked.

'You'll never believe it but a flying saucer came down and whisked them all away,' she said, taking a sip of elderberry wine.

'Sit down, Thelma,' urged Sylvie, 'you've had too much to drink.'

There was an embarrassed silence in which some rearranged themselves on the sofa, some looked out of the window and some rummaged in their pockets for cigarettes.

'No smoking,' Thelma said sternly.

'What about that UFO that was over here, then?' Otley

said. 'A lot of us saw it – chased us like merry hell all over the place.'

'People have been seeing them for centuries,' said Jeff. 'From about twelve hundred and something.'

'Probably blown up their own planets and looking for another,' said Sylvie, handing round Spam sandwiches and potato crisps.

'It's taking them long enough to find one, then.' Thelma said.

'For all we know they might be living here now,' Jeff said, taking a sandwich. 'There's a queer old stick up at Cat-stone.'

I didn't know if I could cope with all this. I was still struggling with the wok. But Otley and Jeff seemed to get on well enough and they arranged to practise some morris dancing the next day. It was a balmy night and we made our way out into the garden to the old summerhouse. The lights of the hamlets were strung out like a necklace all round the base of the hills. Earthlight on the dark side of the moon seemed to glimmer from the inside like a Chinese lantern. Sylvie did a Grecian dance in and out of the rhododendrons, which she had learned when she was five in Mrs Arkwright's Moppets. We applauded politely.

'Why don't you grow up,' Thelma told her.

'Mummy didn't want me to grow up,' said Sylvie petu-lantly.

'Mummy's dead,' said Thelma.

Sylvie began to cry and fled through the bushes towards the house.

'Poor old thing,' I said. 'That was a bit harsh.'

'Her and her namby-pamby ways,' Thelma said. 'I'll murder her one of these days.' She didn't really mean it; she'd been saying that since they were in the Mixed Infants and Sylvie stole one of her ginger biscuits at milk-time. It was only sisterly hate.

The morris men were a jolly lot: Bill, Eddie, Chas, Ron, Wesley and Dick. They were going to do the fertility dance for the harvest festival up on Rombald's Moor, where the hole was. Sylvie could go on first if she liked, warm up the audience for them. If it didn't rain.

'It's a lovely night,' I said, looking up.

'That's the evening star,' said Jeff, pointing at Venus.

We gathered ourselves into a little clump, like the petals of a sleeping dandelion, and gazed at the firmament. There was nothing else to do; the pubs would be closing and there would only be the Open University on television, talking about the function of fossils or the complex transformation of inversion. Not that I'm against that sort of hang-up, if you prefer it to bondage.

'No, it isn't,' Otley said suddenly, 'it's moving!'

What we thought was Venus was moving steadily south in the direction of Hebden Bridge. A glowing, golden cigar-shaped object hovered over Pondon reservoir. Winking lights went out and left a dark mass from which a luminous disc dropped like a stone into the water. We stood mesmerized. Had we seen it or hadn't we?

'I told you they were after our water,' Otley said presently.

'Well, there's plenty of it,' said Thelma, as we turned to go back to the house. Jeff seemed to be thinking hard and said it was too nice to go in so he was going for a stroll. No, he didn't want company. He liked to be on his own sometimes. There was magic in the air and he seemed to be touched with silver: silver-gold hair, silver-blue eyes, silver-grey shirt with the sheen of a fresh-water pearl and silver-brown trousers like the bark of a birch after rain. That must have been when I fell in love with him, as I remembered a favourite poem, something about moonlight:

> . . . A harvest mouse goes scampering by,
> With silver claws, and silver eye;
> And moveless fish in the water gleam,
> By silver reeds in a silver stream.

'He's a mystery, that one,' Bill remarked, as we said goodnight. 'He suddenly appeared from nowhere, as if he'd dropped out of the sky.'

I was up very early the next morning as I wanted to do my diary before we went looking for hedgerow greens for dinner. I found a corner of the wilderness and put down an old coat to sit on. There was a little plastic-topped stool in the kitchen but it made a noise like a whoopee cushion when you sat on it; then there was the deckchair with a broken leg which had to be propped up with the family Bible; or the wooden rocking-chair which somersaulted you over if you leaned too far backwards. I felt I was safer on the ground.

Otley was still asleep when I tiptoed out, snoring in the sleeping bag that he goes all night fishing with. He wants fried rice with prawn balls for dinner – I shall have to make them out of a tin of pilchards. The Third World would give its right arm for pilchards.

6 July 2 AC
Up betimes. A friendly sunbeam my alarm clock as it danced in playfully on the breeze. The caterpillars of the cinnabar moth, in their cheerful black-and-yellow football jerseys, rest on the nodding ragwort as if waiting for their lemons at half-time. Dear Crispin out at dawn, helping a poor farmer with a sick cow. His porridge carelessly cast aside. I must needs eat it myself lest it go to waste. A ladybird lights on my hand. How these wild creatures seem to know a friend. I am inspired.

Ladybird, ladybird,
Why have you got
Little red wings,
And spot after spot?

Can this be Crispin cresting the brow on his hands and knees? I must put out the hyssop tea in readiness for my debilitated love. Chin up, my droopy darling – I am here!

That would do for today. One day I intend to donate my diary to the archives at Bradford. As I was packing up, I heard the clicking of the Geiger counter and found Otley at work in the cabbage patch.

'I'm not eating this lot,' he told me. 'They've got milli-Sieverts.'

'D'you think it's as bad as the Black Death?' I asked.

'Are you trying to be funny?' He inquired, moving on to some runner beans. 'They don't think it's funny in Chernobyl.'

'I know,' I said. 'It's ruined all their cucumbers.'

'Will you pop down the market and get some vegetables there?' he said. 'I don't fancy nettles.'

Balls, I muttered under my breath.

'Did you say something?' he wanted to know.

'I said I've got to make some prawn balls,' I lied.

'You can call in at home and see what they're up to as well.'

'All right,' I said. Anything for a quiet life.

I picked up some spring greens and bamboo shoots from the cheapest stall in the market and then called in to see Mike.

'Have you put the milk bottles out and emptied the rubbish-bin?' was all I could think of to say. He had two companions of neutral gender with thin, scraggy legs made of moulded denim, spiked hair and earrings. They could be anybody. Had they seen the UFO, I wondered. Yes, they had, and everybody was saying how it seemed to stop over High Riding, floodlighting it like Fountains Abbey. We hadn't noticed that at the time, we'd thought it was the moon. The local radio said there had been a lot of activity thereabouts and Mike thought they knew why. Heron, the tall particularly scraggy one with the far-away look in his misty grey eyes, had been studying earth magnetism: ley lines and prehistoric landmarks – stone circles, barrows and the like. He spread a map out on the table and pin-pointed High Riding.

'It's on the cross of ley lines coming over Elbolton to Hebden Bridge, north to south; and again, going east–west over Druid's Altar to Pendle Hill.'

We looked at all the 'x's marking the spots with the biggest 'x' in the middle. Who am I to call him a liar?

'All places of ancient magic,' he went on, 'and High Riding in the centre must be a power point.'

'Oh! dear, I hope not,' I said. 'There's enough trouble as it is, what with British Telecom being privatized, an' that.'

'Better look out, Mum,' Mike grinned, 'in case Scottie beams you up.'

I looked up at him. Tall, dark and handsome. It was true. I had got a son, after all. I looked down. He still hadn't cleaned his baseball boots; it was one of the hazards of being tall – you couldn't see your feet. Yes, they had enough to eat; no, nobody had complained about the noise. Why didn't we go to the Canary Islands with the Co-op? I know when I'm not wanted, so I picked up my shopping to go.

'I'll be off, then,' I said. 'There may be something in what you say, but it all sounds a bit far-fetched to me.'

'Not everything can be measured with a stick,' said the little one, who had not spoken up to now.

'This is Pauline,' Mike said. 'She's our lead vocalist.'

I looked closer. There was not much difference between her and Heron, only in height. They were both sandy-haired and freckled and made sudden angular movements and, yes, she had two little lumps.

'Does your mother know . . . I mean, are you all right?' I said.

'We're all boys together,' she assured me.

'Glad we came – it's given us a good idea for a new number, seeing it all lit up like that on the moors.'

'Silver Riding,' Mike said. 'It'll be a smash hit at the tech.'

'I'm a poet; if you want some words I'd do them,' I volunteered.

There was no answer to that but I'll do them anyway. I already had the refrain buzzing round in my head:

> Silver Riding, Land of the Free,
> Oh! how much you mean to me.

I picked up my bamboo shoots for the second time and made off with them, threading my way through a crowd of sari-clad women talking to Sammy Chandra. They were pointing skywards and chattering excitedly.

'Indeed,' Sammy was telling them, 'the *Ramayana* states categorically that the gods descended to earth in *vimanas* – but I do not know if they are the same thing as flying saucers. My nephew will inform you of it; he has a scientific O Level and reads the *Financial Times*.'

It was true what it said in the encyclopaedia. Gods all came from up there; none of them came out of the ground. Otley was right for once. I must take more notice of him in future. But not to the extent of making real prawn balls; who does he think he is, Paul Getty?

I called in at the library for that book of wartime recipes. Woolton Pie, apricot jam made out of turnips, that sort of thing. I have a recipe for poverty pie but I haven't got any stale cheese. They didn't seem to have what I want. Instead, there were American cookies thick with chocolate and cream; Indian dishes containing ten cloves of garlic and decorated with silver paper; German ones demonstrating sausages cruising in a sea of cabbage; French fish with one eye, lying in a pink sauce like a Picasso painting and raw Swedish herring on pieces of cardboard to be crunched when you come back from your roll in the snow. I would have to invent my own ethnic food.

As I approached High Riding, the clashing of sticks told me the morris men were out practising. I peeped through the trees and saw Otley with his left leg raised and jumping about as if he'd dropped the flat-iron on his foot. With a bit of luck I could get on with my cooking in peace. We would have late dinner like the nobility.

I soon made the prawn balls. I did them à la fish cakes only spherical like gob stoppers. He wouldn't know the difference. I once did the Stork margarine test on him and he thought it was fresh farm butter.

Diced pork; I can use the spam up for that. The Third World would be glad of spam. There was a tin of pineapple chunks in the cupboard. Soy sauce – who do they think I am, Fanny Cradock? HP will have to do. Sliced peppers; I cut up some comfrey leaves, which were hairy but green. The rice had boiled itself into a splodge, now I had to fry it. Everything into the wok; stir it with the cooking chopsticks, drain it on the tempura rack. What a blow – it has to be served up in halves of fresh pineapple! I found a turnip with its leaves still on. What luck! I gouged out the middle and poured some pineapple juice over it. Garnish with a sprig of coriander and it's ready to eat; where am I going to get coriander this side of the bamboo curtain? Parsley's good enough for me. I went out and searched the wilderness but there was no sign of any parsley. There was a nice piece of chickweed that would have to do.

Some dishes the longer they cook, the better they are, but this wasn't one of them. By the time Otley turned up, it looked like wood shavings and dead cockroaches and smelt like burnt rubber tyres.

'I can't eat that pig-swill,' he complained.

'The Third World would be glad of that,' I told him.

'Bugger the Third World,' he said.

'I'll put a tin of Scotch broth in it; it'll be all right,' I said.

'I thought you were doing Chinese cuisine,' he said, offended.

'It is Chinese cuisine,' I said, stirring in the Scotch broth. 'It's just that we're not used to it.'

His eyes began to swivel with a mixture of rage and hunger and I placed myself strategically between him and the chopping-board.

'I'm off down the chip shop,' he said eventually.

'It's all right, I'll go,' I said, eager to get out of the house. 'You look as if you've sprained your ankle or something.'

'It's that clompin', big cart-horse, Wesley – keeps treading on my toes with his bloody big clogs on. I'll pulverize him.'

'I thought you were doing all right,' I lied. 'I saw you through the trees coming up from the village.'

'It's all right for a laugh,' he said. 'You'll have to make me a proper outfit, though, for the fertility dance.'

'What will you want?' I asked anxiously.

'Bells, baldrics and a straw boater with flowers on,' he said.

'I'll have a look in the spastics' shop,' I promised.

'I didn't know spastics wore baldrics,' he said.

'They don't,' I said. 'It's like Oxfam only for English people.'

'I don't know where I'm going to get bells from.' He looked worried.

'You can get them off those reins they make for toddlers,' I told him, 'and from cats' collars.' He still wasn't satisfied.

'He says he wants silver ones,' he mused. That seemed to ring a bell.

I found some black velvet trousers in Oxfam to cut off at the knee, added a strip of Velcro from Woolworths and hey presto! A nifty pair of knickerbockers. Wouldn't he be pleased. The RSPCA was good enough to sell me some cats' collars with bells on. White football socks from the Scouts' Jumble Sale. A cricket shirt from Help the Aged and the local Amateur Dramatics lent me a straw boater, as they'd just finished doing *Three Men in a Boat*. Blue ribbon, four inches wide, from down the market made a good baldric. Buttercups and daisies to put round his hat. He would look jolly!

'Where are the poppies and cornflowers?' he wanted to know.

Baldrics, I thought to myself.

IT WAS A worrying time for us conservationists and we hardly knew which way to turn. Strontium in the milk, caesium in the meat, acid rain coming down from the skies and the danger of radiation from Chernobyl getting into the world's water supply. We knew they'd encased it in concrete but had they caught it in time? Otley worked overtime with his Geiger counter. Had it got as far as Ousel Beck?

'Just make sure everything's well-cooked,' he instructed me. So I decided not to bother with the wok for a day or two until we got used to the idea; I made an earth pie – potatoes, carrots and onions, left to cook in milk for as long as it liked and eaten with grated cheese and spring greens. It was as good as anything.

'You *can* cook if you want to,' Otley said accusingly.

'I have to wait for inspiration,' I said, rather like a genius of the Royal Academy. 'I'm not always in the mood.'

Otley had found a clump of evil-looking rhubarb and put it through the old wooden mangle in the potting-shed to make wine with. He likes rhubarb but he doesn't like the stringy bits that hang down your chin like knitting when you're eating it. Granny always used rhubarb to clean the pans out with; it's better than pan scrubbers.

'It'll be ready to drink by Christmas,' he said, as we carried two plastic buckets up the garden path like Bill and Ben.

We had an apple and a glass of milk, exchanging milk moustaches before we went our separate ways. Otley went up on to the moors with his Geiger counter, looking for contaminated sheep, and I took my diary along the towpath of the Leeds and Liverpool canal. It was hot and sunny with little puffs of cotton wool up in the sky for clouds. I passed the Ancient Britons on their weekly walk – a multi-coloured crocodile stopping to examine hedgerows here, the reed beds there and waving their walking sticks with gay abandon. We would have been with them but for doing-it-ourselves.

'Where are you off to?' I called after them.

'Up the goit,' said Oggy Birkinshaw.

'Down the clough and on to Penistone Way,' shouted Daisy Rimmer.

'Don't do anything I wouldn't do,' I shouted back.

'Too late – we've done it!'

The still-life water of the cut seemed quieter for their passing. I found a shady spot to eat my peanut-butter sandwiches, sitting on a large plastic bag that I'd bought a pillow in. Non-allergic, £2 in the market, four for £7.50.

7 July 2 AC

My friend the sun smiling his warm yellow smile. The stately purple bellflower bowing as I go by; what a charming damsel she is, hanging her head in shame like Princess Di.

A bumble-bee sits drowsing on a thistle. Awake, my furry one! Your children are calling for you! A water vole hurries on to his clandestine abode, eyes like currants in a spotted dick.

> Make haste, little vole,
> Someone's plugged up your hole!

Dear Crispin doing good among his parishioners. How I bless the day he obtained the perpetual curacy of Upper Thump; it is a very paradise. His posset is awaiting his return. Can this be he hobbling along the turnpike, a sack of kindling on his back? He is nearly mown down by a juggernaut. Dear Crispin. He forgot his spectacles.

It seemed to be getting hotter and I became aware of two suns overhead; the second one blinked and then shot off at an angle of ninety degrees in the direction of Penistone Way. It seemed to stop and then fell to the ground like a dead pigeon. I watched until it rose again and continued its journey south. The real sun was still there. Had I been dreaming? Anyway, I wanted to do some painting and I hadn't got my dragonfly yet. I must go and see Thelma.

What turmoil I found at High Riding! Thelma with a strained hamstring and Sylvie with a summer cold. Could I give them a hand? The whatnots wanted dusting and they hadn't eaten for simply ages. Thelma, sitting in the big wing-chair with her left leg up on a footstool, had been told to rest; her beloved safari suit hung nearby on a ladder-back chair so that she could touch it when she needed comforting. Her dark eyes were burning as dull as coke instead of the black diamonds they were and she was wearing an old, green and orange glazed cotton dress, with a hint of the African jungle about it. Beethoven's Fifth Symphony blaring out its victory 'v's. A little smile on her thin, hard lips told me she was unaware of the torment her sister was undergoing. Or perhaps she was secretly enjoying it.

Sylvie, huddled in a pink fluffy dressing gown, red-nosed and snuffling into a paper tissue, jumped to her feet when I came in.

'She's at it again,' she screamed, clutching at my sleeve. 'She knows I can't stand it – she does it on purpose!'

'Never mind,' I soothed. 'I'll make a cup of tea.'

'Shut up, you miserable sod,' said Thelma, 'or I'll put your head down the bloody bog and pull the chain!'

'Would you like toasted tea-cakes with it?' I asked them. Yes, they would, but they went on regardless.

'All that Big Daddy stuff,' Sylvie screeched, 'sitting in that Big Daddy chair listening to Big Daddy music.'

'Shut your gob or I'll shut it for you,' Thelma threatened.

'And would you like some strawberry jam?' I inquired, in an effort to change the subject. Yes they would.

'Walking about in trousers, sleeping in the master bedroom,' Sylvie went on. 'What do you think you are, a Big Daddy?'

'She's got a thing about men with beards as well,' Thelma said.

'And pipes,' said Sylvie. 'Can't stand pipe smokers.'

'She likes fairies,' Thelma sniggered. 'Mummy's little pet.'

'Shut up!' Sylvie screamed.

'Father couldn't do anything with her,' Thelma explained. 'She screamed the place down every time he came near her.'

'He had a beard like that picture of Moses crossing the Red Sea,' Sylvie said. 'I thought he was going to drown me with the kittens.'

'She wouldn't go near a bucket till she was twelve,' Thelma said.

Recriminations went back and forth like a ping-pong ball. Fending and proving Granny used to call it. A family game more often played than 'Consequences'. Then when Sunday came, the mint humbugs would be handed round and everybody went to chapel and made out they were good.

As I tidied up the kitchen I found myself idly wondering if there was any washing-up in space. Or did they use paper cups and then throw them out? There was always a pile of them in the park. The two ugly sisters were still at it next door like peevish poodles. That would be one advantage of space – with a goldfish bowl on their heads, you wouldn't hear them.

Thelma said there was a dragonfly in the British Moths drawer, next to the spotted burnets. She caught it by accident as they had no wings to speak of, she said, so she didn't bother with them. I opened all the drawers of the dresser where she kept her collection as the labels had long since faded. Spotted burnets all right, but no dragonfly. Oh, well. I could do a spotted burnet riding on the clappers. Same difference.

'Yes, Cinderella can go to the ball,' Jeff said, when he came into the kitchen looking for boil-in-the-bag stuff for their dinner. The lads were busy in the vegetable plot, trying to get rid of all the pests first before they could eat anything. Slugs, carrot fly, club root, aphids – everything got at it before they did.

'You can make insecticides out of nicotine,' I told him.

'It doesn't make sense,' he said. 'Give yourself lung cancer so you don't pollute the atmosphere with chemicals.'

'They get you every way,' I agreed.

The lads had decided to let me be first reserve for the fertility dance. Ron might not be able to make it. His wife was expecting their third in August and it looked like tempting fate. Otley could step into his place with a bit more practice and I could stand by in case somebody broke a leg. I wouldn't have to write to the Queen, after all. The afternoon sun streamed through the stained glass, illuminating Jeff like one of the knights of the Round Table in the old chapel window. He rested his hand lightly on my shoulder. I felt a tingle.

'See you tomorrow, then,' he said, with another of his winks. What did he mean? In the space of a second he had changed from a Lancelot to a music-hall comedian.

I took Sylvie some hot whisky-and-lemon and Thelma thought she had recovered enough to hop into the kitchen later on if they wanted anything. Sylvie was knitting a scarf with a blue budgie perched on the end of one of the needles.

'Who's a pretty boy, then?' she kept saying, as she knitted away. 'He likes his little see-saw.'

'I couldn't find the dragonfly,' I told Thelma.

'Well, there was one in there. I saw it on Saturday,' she said.

'Say hello to Auntie May,' Sylvie said, holding the bird up on a knitting needle.

'Hello,' I said. 'I didn't know you had a budgie.'

'This is Tinkerbell; he flies up to Never Never Land with Peter Pan,' she said. 'He lives in Mummy's room with me.'

Thelma raised her eyes heavenwards and held out her hand. 'I'll have some of that whisky,' she said.

'Tinkie, have a little drinkie,' Sylvie twittered to the unsuspecting bird as she dipped its beak into the whisky. He went out like a light and fell off the knitting needle on to her lap.

'Silly bugger,' said Thelma.

I made my escape after arranging to come dancing on the morrow. Otley would be home soon for his jacket potatoes and greens and I had promised to do his costume that night. I was just wondering what I could make out of withering bamboo shoots when the Geiger counter came clicking down the garden path.

'Did you see it?' Otley wanted to know as soon as he got in.

'That UFO?' I replied, as I set the table. 'I was just eating my sandwiches down the cut.'

'I met the Ancient Britons wandering about in a daze,' he said. 'They were right up the goit one minute and the next minute they were on Penistone Crags; they don't know how they got there.'

'It's a funny how d'you do,' I said.

'Oggy Birkinshaw said he was telling Daisy about his holiday in Morocco then suddenly he was on the crags talking to Nellie Outram about her old man's prostate.'

Somebody was trying to tell us something but we weren't sure who.

We switched on the box but there was no mention of the incident on the regional news, which didn't surprise Otley. It was official policy not to recognize UFOs, just as the National Health Service doesn't recognize allergies; if they did, they would have to treat them and they've got enough trouble treating things you can see.

'They don't want panic in the streets,' he said.

'And we were the last to hear about Edward and Mrs Simpson,' I reminded him, as I put out a basket of apples and oranges.

'Haven't you made any pudding?' he inquired, crestfallen.

'I thought we were doing-it-ourselves,' I said.

'No need to go that far,' he said. 'You never know when to stop.'

We spent the rest of the evening cutting bells off cats' collars and then I sewed them on to arm and leg ribbons. Velcro round the sawn-off trousers to make them into knee breeches. A cummerbund and a baldric. Flowers on the hat and hey presto! A morris man. Fetching, but then Rambo leaves me cold.

'Let *me* try it now,' I begged.

'What for?' he asked in disbelief.

'Supposing you get kidnapped by a flying saucer,' I said. 'The show must go on.'

It didn't fit properly, of course. The baldric was too long and kept tripping me up; the breeches fastened round my ankles; the hat fell over my eyes and the shirt looked like wet washing flapping on the line. Otley turned his back and his shoulders heaved. Was he laughing or crying?

'A tuck here and there and it'll be all right,' I said.

I couldn't help noticing that when he put his arm round my shoulder there was no tingle. We sat in the put-u-up to watch some television, like the couple in Orwell's *Nineteen Eighty-Four* – side by side but unaware of each other. Big Brother watching us in the corner. How do we know that Sir Robin Day's not a KGB man with a two-way mirror?

It was some time before I realized we were holding hands. He must have thought it was Bella. Well, I could pretend it was Jeff. Murder and mayhem in the deep South; debasement in the delta; sweating in the swamp. Why do we waste our time like this? I could be knitting a dish-cloth; Otley could be sawing logs for our Norwegian wood-burning stove. No, that was Crispin. That reminds me, I've got to paint some ladybirds. Otley was snoring now and I slid my hand slowly out of his and switched the television off.

'I was watching that,' he said.

'I thought you were asleep,' I said, putting the box on again.

'Sneaking off to bed in case I want some supper,' he said accusingly.

'I'm not stopping you having any supper,' I said.

'You're supposed to do it. You're the Mummy.'

Did he mean it or was he laughing at me? There were times when I wished I was a black widow spider – I'd have bitten his head off long ago.

I made some sandwiches and cocoa while he watched a red-triangle film on Channel Four. I avoided looking at it as far as possible. I remember going to see what we thought was an educational film in London because everybody was dressed in white coats, but it turned out to be a lot of Swedes measuring their things; it put me off my choc-ice, I can tell you.

And what the *Kama Sutra* has to do with religion I don't know, but the Hindus have got it all round their temples; no wonder their deities have all got two pairs of hands. Mind you, their churches are a lot fuller than ours; I'm ready to concede it might have something to do with it.

And Great Aunt Adelaide once brought me *The Perfumed Garden* back from Norwich; she thought it was about the Old English Lavender fields in East Anglia. What a shock that was, and us Primitive Methodists! It's not safe to go abroad.

Otley thinks I'm frigid, but they said that about Queen Victoria for covering her piano legs up; they'll say anything. He once went to the Marriage Guidance Council and complained he wasn't getting his conjugal rights, but I went and told them he was getting them round the pub. He was very annoyed.

To be honest, I wouldn't mind being one of three hundred and sixty-five concubines. Only once a year and as much Turkish Delight as you can eat. Diplomatic immunity for shoplifting in Harrods. It's the life of Riley.

Otley was wide awake now and was viewing naked bodies writhing on black satin sheets like serpents hatching in a heap of compost.

'That reminds me,' he said, 'I've got to get some more maggots. I'm going fishing tomorrow.'

I walked sideways into the kitchen with my back to the television set to show my disapproval. He needn't get any ideas.

'Who wants to watch that?' I sniffed.

'I do,' he said. 'I wonder if they do it in space.'

'What, with those silver suits and goldfish bowls on?' I said.

'I'm not going, then,' he said emphatically.

'I expect they have to do it before they set off and then again when they get back,' I said. 'If they're not too tired.'

'The nearest star is 4.2 million miles away,' Otley said, looking at his factfinder. 'It's a long time to wait.'

'I wonder if they have silver babies,' I said, thinking of Jeff.

'Like them you hang on the Christmas tree?' inquired Otley.

'Mmm,' I murmured dreamily.

'Search me,' he said.

The heaving flesh had come to a standstill and Otley looked bereft. He tried another channel but with no luck; it was *Their Lordships' House* again. He muttered something about poncing bloody perverts and switched off. Would I like a little drink, he wondered, as he ruffled my hair playfully. Suddenly I had a splitting headache and I began to search frantically for his Mogadons.

'What are you looking for?' he wanted to know.

'I'm looking for your telescope,' I lied. 'I want to look at the Moon.'

'It's here,' he said, fishing it out of his rucksack, and we spent a boring ten minutes trying to find the Oceanus Procellarum.

'I'm off, then. See you tomorrow,' I said. I don't know why I should feel guilty. It's not my fault Bella's gone to Majorca.

As I am the Mummy, I had to be up early the next morning to wave my hero off with his sandwiches and live yoghurt. He took the old banger as he was too early to use his free bus pass and he had not had any tablets since the UFOs came into our lives and cured his *malaise*. But I don't know which is worse, Otley with or without *malaise*.

'Hurry up!' he kept urging, as he ate his muesli and sun-dried raisins. I scampered round the kitchen looking for the staff of life and something to put on it.

'Don't overdo it,' he warned. 'Remember the Third World.'

'D'you want a tin of rice pudding, then?' I inquired.

He leapt up from the table in a fury and began throwing everything into a waxed paper-bag out of a cornflakes packet. Bread, cheese, tomatoes, bean sprouts, pickled onions, sardines, yoghurts, apples, bar of chocolate, sticking plasters, a Swiss Army knife and a packet of Fisherman's Friend throat lozenges.

'What are you going to drink?' I asked.

'This,' he said, throwing in a can of lager and two cartons of milk.

'You've not left me any,' I protested.

'You're a selfish little madam,' he said.

I escorted him to his chariot, carrying the crackling, lucky-dip under my arm, while he checked the surrounding vegetation for milliSieverts. The air was damp and humid and the moor rose out of the mist like Fujiyama in a Japanese brush painting.

'It's going to be hot,' I said conversationally.

'How do you know?' he said.

'If you're not back in time for the dance practice I'll take your place,' I said hopefully.

'I'll be back,' he said, slamming the car door.

'And Myrtle wants us to call in sometime to see her new avocado bathroom suite with bidet and co-ordinated, total-look bedroom.'

'I've got a total-look bedroom as well,' he said. 'Total chaos!'

He started up the engine and began to move off, scattering gravel in all directions. I gave him my best Mummy-like wave.

'Mind you don't fall in,' I lied. 'I don't want you to get pneumonia. Free!' I said, skipping down the garden path like the genie coming out of his bottle in *The Arabian Nights*. Away, dull care, I can turn a somersault, stand on my head or go back to bed. Anything I like. After sweeping up the muesli and bean sprouts and mopping up the yoghurt – a pot of yoghurt goes a long way when it's splattered against the wall – making the beds and scouring the sink, I decided to be a gracious lady. I was too tired to turn cartwheels.

I gave myself a shower by standing in the tin bath and tipping a watering can over my head, then threw the water over some hydrangeas as they're always thirsty, I'm told.

The sun soon dried my hair and I looked for a silk handkerchief to polish it with but couldn't find one, so I used my
nylon headscarf instead. The result was slightly different.
Where it was supposed to lie smooth and shining it stood on
end with static electricity and I had to flatten it down with
the sunflower oil we had bought for wokking. It was still a
good colour, goldy brown; we didn't go grey in our family,
we just dropped down dead and then the world realized
how old we were. A dusting of powder over my freckles and
a spot of eye shadow so that I don't look like Henry Tudor
counting his money. A trace of pink lipstick. Don't want to
look like Madame Butterfly waiting for the US Navy to
appear on the horizon. My old jeans lay dejected in a
corner; it was time they were replaced but, oh! the confusion
of sizes and all about ten feet long! Jeans from India and
Taiwan, from China and Hong Kong; jeans from all around
the globe, going for a song! I donned the grey bombazine
skirt and a broderie anglaise blouse, the colour of Wall's
Cornish ice cream with age. My straw hat and Dorothy bag
containing a lace handkerchief and a stick of frozen eau-de-
Cologne, in case I got the vapours, completed my ensemble.
I picked up my diary and a bamboo pen with a tassel on
that I got with a silk address book made in Shanghai, and I
sauntered out feeling like the Madwoman of Chaillot.

I passed a herd of black-and-white Friesians, which
looked anxiously at me and then gathered together round
an electricity pylon, preferring to be electrocuted than have
anything to do with a woman in a big hat. Five cats, three
horses, two hounds straining at the leash and sixteen feathered friends later, I arrived at a field full of buttercups and
daisies and sat down to do my diary.

8 July 2 AC
Up betimes to wash my face in the moring dew. Dear
Crispin strewed our chamber with sweet woodruff and wild

thyme ere he ventured out to rescue Dobbin stuck with his two front legs over the wire netting. The foxgloves nodding in the breeze ... whisht! I can hear those fairy bells a-tinkling merrily, calling the little people to their fairy business. I weave a chain of pink-tipped daisies to adorn my brow as a startled bunny pricks up her ears and then lollops away.

> Run, Mrs Moppity,
> Ears all floppity,
> Crookedy legs,
> Going hoppity, hoppity.

Methinks it is near time my beloved partook of a little repast; his gruel is awaiting in the bain-marie. But stay! It seems that Dobbin is now abroad and that Crispin is stuck with his legs in the wire netting. Dear Crispin. I needs must sally forth to Woolworths to purchase some wire-cutters.

I was just picking a giant puff-ball to stir-fry in the wok when I became aware of a whirring noise coming from behind a hillock. I crawled up to the top hardly daring to breathe and peered over the ridge. There was a strange craft made of shiny metal and shaped like an upturned pie-dish, about the length of a bus and with what looked like port-holes round the middle. A blue light shone inside and I could see shapes moving around. A silver-clad figure stood on the grass and seemed to be looking for something. Suddenly he saw me and pointed in my direction with a stick. I wanted to scream and run but it was as if I were paralysed and struck dumb. I watched as he got back into the machine and then it was gone. I felt a sudden blast of hot air that sent me rolling head over heels down the hillock and I found myself at the bottom holding a very squashed puff-ball. Perhaps I could put it in a sandwich.

I looked around for some dock leaves to rub on my blistered hands and kept the young tender ones to make a dock pudding with. I had also promised to make flowerpot loaves and would have to empty two pots of geraniums before I could start. *Chapatis* would be easier: you just smack them a few times to flatten them and put them on a hot stone till you want them. I must have a word with Sammy Chandra.

I was still trembling from my close encounter of the third kind when I met Jimmy One Eye waving his arms like a windmill: frog shaped, dung-smeared, his good eye raking the horizon like a Cyclops, two cauliflower ears, apple cheeks and a nose like an old potato baked on the bonfire. A primeval bog man like Pete Marsh and the Tollund Man only he was still alive. The Brooklimes had farmed this land for centuries and did a bit of weaving on the side here, a bit of skulduggery there. When everybody died of the Black Death, the Black Death died of the Brooklimes. The plague swept through Low Riding, stopped dead when it met Old Ranter Brooklime and was never seen again.

'Don't come by 'ere again wi' that bloody 'at on; you've scared old Blossom out of 'er wits. She's laid out there wi' 'er legs up as if she's been hit by a thunderbolt!' He seemed to be addressing me.

'They were standing under that pylon when I came past,' I told him. 'Do you think she's been electrocuted?'

'No she 'ant,' he snapped, 'they allus stand there, they likes the 'umming noise – it keeps 'em company.'

'I tiptoed past so as not to turn the milk sour,' I said lamely.

'If they sees owt peculiar, that's it!' he said.

I realized then it must have been the flying saucer. I'd read about horses stampeding, dogs going mad, canaries losing their whistle and a cow found with a hole in its side and all the blood drained out of it. I'd better not say that, though.

'It must have been the flying saucer,' I said.

'The what?'

'It was behind that hillock down in Boggle's field – by the railway,' I added, as if that made it easier to believe.

'Oh, aye!'

'I saw it,' I went on. 'It was as big as a double-decker only round.'

'An' did you see a little green man?' he jeered.

'No, it was a silver one,' I said. 'He was on the ground looking for something in the long grass.'

'I expect he'd lost 'is contact lenses,' he said.

'I tried to scream but I couldn't; he froze me with a stick and I couldn't move till they'd gone.' I showed him my blistered hands, the grass stains on my blouse, my buckled hat, the mangled puff-ball. But he was not convinced. His eye cauterized me like a laser.

'Are you one o' them lot up at the big 'ouse?' he said at last.

'Only for a week or two,' I said. 'We're doing-it-ourselves.'

'I might 'ave known. It's like a loony bin up there at times; they want lockin' up, the lot of 'em.'

I panicked as he came towards me with a broken pitch-fork he had picked up out of the ditch.

'My 'usband's a lunatic, Mr One Eye,' I said, copying his manner of speaking, 'but I'm not – I'm just an ornery 'ousewife an' I allus donkey-stone the doorstep on a Friday.' Surely he recognized me.

'My name's Brooklime,' he said. 'James Brooklime.'

'I know, your Dirk's a friend of my Mike,' I said simperingly.

'Well,' he said, moving aside to let me pass, 'jus' don't come round 'ere again wi' that bloody 'at on, that's all.'

I trudged wearily up the moor to High Riding, the afternoon sun behind me picking out the hedges and dry-stone walling like cross-stitches in a sampler. I clutched my diary and my bamboo pencil close to my heart. There might be time to paint some ladybirds before Otley got back from the dancing practice. It was hard trying to be an Edwardian lady with all this going on; and I wondered idly, if I got into a flying saucer dressed like this, would it blow my skirt up over my head like it used to do on the cakewalk at the Whitsuntide Fair?

It was clouding over when Otley came home with his catch, a little brown trout, hardly worth ending up smelling like a polecat for.

'I'll have it stuffed with mushrooms,' he said, laying it out on the chopping-board and standing back to admire it.

'There's this puff-ball,' I said, holding it out.

'It looks like a dead Yorkshire pudding,' Otley complained. 'What's happened to it?'

'I sat on it when I saw the flying saucer,' I had to confess.

I told him the whole story while he prepared the fish and wrapped it into a neat parcel ready for the oven. I averted my eyes from these obscene goings on; since turning vegetarian I get nightmares about fishmongers and butchers.

'Next time you see them, ask them what they want,' Otley urged.

'All right,' I agreed.

'And where they've come from,' he went on.

'I'll ask if they want a cup of tea,' I said brightly.

'Don't be ridiculous,' he said. 'They'll live on tablets.'

'I'll give them one of your Mogadons,' I then suggested.

'You don't want me to turn into a werewolf and be out all night, do you?' he said, carrying his trout over to the oven.

'Wait a minute,' I cried. 'The flowerpot bread's in there.'

He paced about like a captive king of the jungle until I opened the oven door and extracted the flowerpots. Something was wrong. They each had a long tail on where the dough had run out through the hole. I tipped them out and held one up like a stick of candyfloss. I nibbled at it cautiously and it just tasted hot.

'It'll be all right when it's cold,' I reassured him.

'Can't you do anything right!' he scolded.

'Well, it doesn't say you've got to plug up the holes,' I said.

He snorted as he put his parcel carefully in the middle of the oven and sat down to keep watch.

'I daren't leave it with you,' he said, shaking his head.

I broke off the tails from the flowerpot loaves and held them up in triumph. One should always turn defeat into victory.

'Look!' I said. 'We've got two French sticks for the soup.'

We had a modest meal that evening. Hedgerow broth to start with, then Otley had trout and I had fried puff-ball and tomato ketchup. I went upstairs while Otley took off his smelly clothes and had a watering-can shower, in case he asked me to wash his back. There was enough water in the big jug and bowl to make myself respectable and I changed into a blue-and-white gingham frock and tied my hair in two bunches like the heroine of *Seven Brides for Seven Brothers*. It's true what they say about second childhood and it's like falling in love for the first time all over again.

'You get sillier as you get older,' Otley observed when I went down.

'It's just a bit of fun,' I lied.

Otley wore his checked shirt from the army-surplus stores. He thinks he looks like Paul Newman in *Cool Hand Luke*. The moon was coming up to full, round and white like a Wensleydale cheese as we threaded our way through the shrubbery. Sylvie fluttered us in.

'You be the Tom Fool,' Jeff said, steering me to one side as he arranged the others in pairs. There was that tingle again.

'What's that?' I inquired.

'You collect the money and hit people with a bladder on a stick.'

Wesley played the concertina and they did 'Nancy's Fancy' and 'Mrs Casey', now and then boxing each other's ears.

'That's supposed to be behind the head not a clip on the ear 'ole,' Jeff reminded them. 'Let's have it again till we get it right.'

Otley called a halt when he got earache and they changed over to one entitled 'Young Collins' that required clashing sticks.

'Now watch this one,' their leader warned. 'There's some tricky sticking.'

This was sex discrimination, I thought, as I stood on the sidelines admiring Jeff, but nice with it! Otley gave his partner a black eye with an ill-timed stick and the pattern of dance was switched to the 'Monk's March'.

'Don't forget the double clap before the half hey,' said Jeff.

When they had worn themselves out stamping, clapping and sticking they fell higgledy-piggledy on to the old sofa and lay gasping like a flounder of fat aunts at Blackpool. All except Jeff. There was something different about him. It was as if he had a magnetic field around him and when I got inside it I couldn't pull myself away. It was not a physical sensation, more a psychic power, as though he held the universe in his eyes and looking into them unlocked the secrets of the stars. Jeff the morris man was hiding something.

I sat on the pouffe as close to him as I dared without melting. I hadn't got dressed up like this just to play the Tom Fool. The Chinese lamp behind us threw rainbow-coloured light into the far corners of the room and made lurking shadows on the ceiling.

'Did you see the UFO this afternoon?' I asked casually.

Sylvie came with some tea and Thelma limped after her with sandwiches, putting them down on the coffee-table.

'Help yourselves,' she said, sitting down near her safari suit. 'They say it went over Brandt's and stopped all the machinery.'

'It came down in Boggle's field and I saw it,' I told them.

'Get away,' said Chas. 'It's that old caravan he's got down there.'

'No, it was round.' I said, munching on a pickled onion.

'She's at a funny age,' I heard Bill whisper to Eddie.

'You believe me, don't you?' I said, turning to Jeff and letting my hand fall across his knee. It felt hard. Had he got a wooden leg?

'Of course,' he said. 'Lots of people have seen 'em.'

'Responsible people,' Otley put in, 'like highway patrol-men.'

'Not only me,' I added.

'Where d'you reckon they come from, then?' Chas wanted to know. 'And how do they get about, nipping in and out like that?'

'Patrick Moore'll know on *The Sky at Night*,' Sylvie mused.

'Or Judith Hann on *Tomorrow's World*,' said Thelma.

'They most likely come from group G and K stars within five parsecs of the sun; Tau Ceti, a G type, and Epsilon Eridani, a K type, would be my guess,' Jeff intoned as if in a trance.

'Who told you that?' I asked, looking into his face. Our eyes locked and I felt that I was on the edge of a great adventure.

'I went to night school,' he said and the spell was broken. Otley said it was getting late and we had to go so I dragged myself away.

'I'll test him for milliSieverts next time I come over,' he said.

THE NEXT DAY we went mushrooming in case Otley caught another trout and I showed him where the flying saucer had landed. There was a circle of scorched grass with triangular holes made in the ground; plants had been pulled up leaving patches of bare earth.

'They're testing them for radiation,' said Otley.

'I bet Jeff knows something about it,' I observed. 'They said it was funny how he suddenly appeared at Catstones.'

'Who did?' Otley wanted to know.

'The lads,' I said, getting a fleeting image of a band of marauding Vikings dressed in flowered hats and jingle bells.

'You showed me up last night making sheep's eyes,' he said.

'I'm only doing it in the cause of science,' I lied. 'Sort of market research – it's all the fashion now.'

He turned and gave me a sideways look green with suspicion. His face was lean and unshaven. We were both getting thin with doing it ourselves. He wore a worried frown from wrestling with himself – whether to lose a chattel in order to gain scientific knowledge, or surrender the secrets of the stars to keep his own personal messenger-boy.

'Just don't ponce me, that's all,' he said at last.

'What about Bella?' I asked.

'That's different,' he said.

'I've put up with your hanky-panky for as long as I can remember,' I told him, taking a deep breath. 'Now I'll put my cards on the table.'

'Well?' he inquired, as he stooped to pick a large horse-mushroom.

'Either I go up in a flying saucer or I put a knife in your back,' I said, as if it were the roller-coaster at Shipley Glen.

'You can go in a flying saucer,' he said.

'No hard feelings?' I said.

'No,' he replied.

'We can still be friends, can't we?' I asked.

'Mind you come back, though!' he cautioned. 'You haven't finished that cable-stitch pullover yet.'

'Bella can finish it if I don't come back,' I told him, with the growing confidence of a big carving-knife behind me.

'She can't knit,' he said.

'We don't want to part after all this time,' I went on. 'We can go our own ways in secret like royalty; they manage all right.'

'Yes,' he agreed.

'And Mike's at an awkward age,' I said.

'He always is,' Otley complained.

'You've been there a long time. I'd miss you,' I said, feeling guilty.

'And me,' he said. 'It'd be like when we got rid of the old wooden mangle for that sterilized, operating-theatre job.'

We went the long way home so as not to invade Brooklime

territory, following the beck through Hob Wood and out at the back of our kitchen garden. We could take a cabbage up to High Riding to stir-fry instead of seaweed and there was half a jar of Marmite that would come in handy. Barbara Cartland helped to save the starving Welsh with Marmite just before the war.

'I'll pop in and see how they're doing,' I said, dead-heading a rose or two on the way. Otley trailed behind me. You could see he was only killing time until Bella came back from Majorca.

'Thanks, Dad,' Mike said, taking the bag of mushrooms. 'We can put them in a tin of soup and make creamed mushrooms on toast.'

'Where's Pauline?' I inquired, as Heron came into the kitchen wearing a satin kimono, long beads and a crinkly wig. Was he a transvestite? Otley's fists clenched and he went over to the window.

'She's gone home. She's jealous,' Mike explained.

'What of?' I inquired, but dreading the answer.

'I dunno,' he said, spreading his arms like a Frenchman.

'We haven't got a vocalist now,' Heron explained, 'so I'm doing it on a temporary basis. The audience likes a bit of fancy dress.'

Plausible deniability strikes again. I decided to believe them for now but made a mental note to pick up some AIDS leaflets from the health centre and push them through the letter-box at midnight. They wouldn't know it was me. I went quickly through the rooms on the pretext of rounding up dirty washing. Everything seemed to be in order. Two unmade beds; two piles of sheets on the floor; two lots of mugs and plates on two bedside tables in two different rooms. That spoke for itself. Unless there was a connecting door. A priest's hidey-hole. Something we had overlooked in the thirty-five years we had lived there. It did happen. Secret panels. Blocked up windows. Hidden staircases. I knocked on the walls and rattled all the doorknobs. Lifted up the carpet on the landing and peeped through the cracks in the floorboards.

'Looking for something, Mum?' Mike said suddenly.

'I thought I heard mice,' I said, with great presence of mind.

'That was me brushing my teeth,' he said.

I made some tea and found a tin of flapjacks that are supposed to keep for ever but it was a bit like eating soldered gravel dipped in fish-glue. They'd been up to see if Dirk Brooklime was free to join them, as he used to be in 'Steam' with Mike and his current group was breaking up. Sid was joining 'Signal Box', Harry was joining 'Dandelion Soup' and Wayne was going to London for a trial with 'Send Me a Postcard from Clacton'.

'How is Dirk these days?' I inquired.

'All right,' Mike said, 'but he says there was a madwoman up there yesterday frightening the cows to death.'

'Did he say what she looked like?' I was curious to know.

'She had a funny hat on, staring eyes, wild hair all over the place and a long frock, like a female impersonator.'

'What was she doing, then?' I asked.

'His Dad caught her coming back, all covered in grass, mad as a hatter, he said. Gave a false name – said it was you.' He put his cup down and gave me a sidelong look, just like his father but darker. Where Otley's eyes are green, Mike's are black and mine are faded to go with my hair. It must be something to do with my great-grandmother running off with a Hungarian gypsy. There was that photo of grandad with gold earrings and a kerchief knotted round his neck. Mike must be what you call a throwback and a bit of a puzzle to us.

'It was me!' I confessed. They were not at all surprised.

They listened with interest to my story of the flying saucer and my plans to go up in one if I got the chance.

Heron talked about them following ley lines and using the earth's magnetic poles. It sounded a lot of nonsense but I'm nothing if not impartial. I disbelieve in everything equally. Until I find out.

'You've got your free bus pass,' said Mike. 'Why d'you want to bother with flying saucers?'

'Because they're there,' I said, like men who climb mountains.

'Well, mind you don't fall out,' he said, dismissing the subject.

They had to practise their new number 'Silver Riding' so we made our exit as we didn't want perforated eardrums. Yes, they knew how to work the washing-machine. No, they wouldn't forget to pick up the trail of potato peelings that the dustmen left. Thomas Cook was doing a special, reduced package-tour to the Dodecanese. Wouldn't we like to go to Cos, where the lettuces come from?

'We can get a Cos lettuce down the market,' Otley told him.

As we were there, we thought we might as well go and see Sammy Chandra and find out what the stars foretold. The Christmas decorations had lost some of their dazzle in the afternoon sun but inside was an Aladdin's cave, a flamboyant mixture of east and west: Nottingham lace tablecloths and a silver platter; Bengal brass and English bone china; West Riding woollens and fine, gold-embroidered silks; the goddess Lakshmi on the wall next to Queen Elizabeth and Mahatma Gandhi; Mrs Thatcher on the other wall with Shiva and Ronald Reagan; little gods consorting with woolly sheep on a fold-up picnic table; and all the perfumes of Arabia spiked with *garam masala*.

'You are going on a long journey,' Sammy informed me, after studying his various bits of paper. 'August is a good time for travel.'

'Where am I going to?' I inquired flippantly, 'Skegness or somewhere?'

'That I cannot predict with any certainty,' he said, his hooked nose casting a shadow on the wall. 'One can only indicate the trends; it is for the gods to decide further.'

'I've not booked anywhere,' I said.

'There is no necessity to obtain a ticket,' he went on, 'with Mars in conflict with the Moon you will be conducted by a whirlwind.'

'How d'you know that?' I asked anxiously.

'There is great consternation and then . . .' He paused for a while.

'And then what?'

'And then silence.'

'Silence! What does that mean?' I said, getting a bit worried.

'Only for a time and then the consternation returns.'

Thank goodness for that, I thought. I cannot imagine life without consternation.

'Anything for me?' Otley wanted to know.

'Oh! Mr Craven,' Sammy said, 'as ever, there is great confusion for one born in an eclipse. To complicate things also, you were born on the cusp and cannot make up your mind whether you are a goat or a water-carrier; it is an insurmountable problem best left to the gods.'

'How much is that?' I asked, feeling in my handbag.

'Two pounds and there is a free gift of a recipe for *rogan josh*.'

'Thanks,' I said, 'and have you got one for *chapatis*?'

'Cheerio,' said Otley, as he dragged me away by the scruff.

'If you call again next week I will give you the solution to your problems,' Sammy called after us as he took off his forecasting coat and put on a velvet jacket.

'You will?' inquired Otley, with renewed interest.

'Without a doubt,' said Sammy. 'We Brits have to stick together.'

'See you next week, then,' I said, looking at the mile-long recipe unfolding in my hand.

'And look out for those bloody wok-wallahs,' he said.

We hopped on a Hoppa to take us into Keighley to collect the magic ingredients. The diced goat was difficult to obtain, so we got some soya chunks instead. Ginger, garlic, asafoetida, cumin, almonds, turmeric, poppy seeds, cayenne pepper, cloves, cardamom, peppercorns, *garam masala* and coriander both ground and fresh, live yoghurt and ghee. We had some dead yoghurt and margarine if that was any use.

The supermarket was buzzing like a beehive: battered bottles, clanking tins and triumphant tills ringing with the sound of money music; young mothers pushing trolleys piled up with children, soap powder, cornflakes and bottles of pop crashing into each other as if they were on the dodgems; an expectant humming throughout as shoppers find money-off coupons and competitions for holidays in Singapore, Barbados, Yugoslavia, Hong Kong and Torremolinos.

'There's one here for a trip to Disneyland,' I said. 'You've only got to get a packet of dog biscuits.'

'I don't want to go to soddin', bloody Disneyland!' snapped Otley.

After we had waited fifteen minutes at the check-out Otley grabbed the basket and dumped it on the floor.

'I'll go round the chip shop,' he said.

We strolled through the shopping precinct, which was in the process of having a glass roof and hanging baskets added to make it into a mall. Giant Rombald had been cleaned up and stood like a man made of plasticine, looking slightly ashamed of himself. It's a handy little town. Everything you want for life clustered round the town square and a peep of the moors at every street corner. Sturdy stone terraces marching up the hillsides, radiating out from the centre like the spokes of a wheel; sprawling council estates with graffiti and bicycle sheds; genteel semis with patios and carports; and brooding Gothick with overgrown gardens and conservatories, standing aloof from the riff-raff.

'There used to be a cherry tree there,' I said, looking at a hole in the ground. One by one trees were disappearing like victims in a whodunnit. Eglantine gouged out to make way for a trim privet hedge. Two ancient poplars executed to straighten out a wall. An old apple tree murdered to make a neat green square of grass.

'I expect that's what they're worried about,' Otley said.

'Who?' I asked.

'The flying saucers.'

'I wonder if they've got trees up there,' I speculated idly.

'Don't be stupid,' he said.

We stopped to look at a clump of horsetail growing out of a wall, its spiky leaves like straggling spiders' legs. I picked a piece and examined it to take back for my diary.

'Myrtle says it's good for gallstones,' I told him.

'Julian Pettifer says it's been here from the year dot,' he said.

'I know,' I said, putting it in my handbag.

'Well, don't kill it after all this time,' he said, snatching it from me.

Bella should be back in a day or two and we could take up our own private lives again like Edward VII and Queen Alexandra.

'I'm only going to paint it,' I assured him.

'Have some respect for the wonders of nature,' he scolded.

'I have, I have,' I said.

'It looks like it,' he said sarcastically.

'You don't mind murdering cucumbers when you feel like it to put them in vinegar,' I said in exasperation. It was always my fault. Same thing with Eleanor of Aquitaine.

Her husband blamed her for their sons revolting when she was locked up in a tower all the time. It's always Mum's fault.

'You won't be told, will you?' he said.

'I'm fed up with you bossing me about!' I shouted.

'You're not normal,' he shouted back. 'A proper wife would be at home making gingerbread men and coconut castles.'

'Clogs!' I said, trying to swear like an Edwardian lady.

'You're a nasty little piece of work when you're that way out,' he said, shaking me violently like a rag doll. I brought my knee up like they show you in the 'Assertive Woman' classes and he began to spin round like a whirling dervish. Just then a Hoppa came in sight and I was able to hop on it before he straightened up.

'You wait till I get home,' I think he was mouthing.

I was packed in the Hoppa like a sardine with old ladies coming back from the Bingo Hall chattering excitedly about their near-misses. We rounded each bend with arms waving like the Keystone Kops in old black and white movies. I thought longingly of outer space. Just me and Jeff in our flying saucer doing the 'Blue Danube' waltz in and out of the galaxies. Pouring out the silver tea. 'One lump or two?' I would say, as I dropped silver cubes of sugar into little silver cups. Jeff would be at the controls like Captain Kirk, avoiding meteors and asteroids with one hand and fighting off space bandits with the other, while I gasped admiringly wearing my see-through ensemble.

It was good to smell fresh air again when I got out on the road up to High Riding. It was like coming out of jail. I might have time to do my diary before the master got home. I don't know what he said he was going to do to me but I kept a bottle of milk handy just in case. You're not allowed to murder your husband with a knife or a gun, but it's all right if you use a bottle of milk or a knitting needle. I washed and changed into a fawn linen skirt and a cotton top and rubbed my fevered brow with eau de Cologne. Oh! dear! What would Crispin think of all this? I feared he would excommunicate me.

9 July 2 AC

My beloved away at dawn's early light to comfort a poor pauper of this parish with a leaking overflow pipe. The blackbird on yonder bough trills me a merry lay; I cool my aching feet in the babbling brook, where a yellow flag stands sentinel like an oriental Coldstream Guard. A still, silent pool hides a great crested newt and the long grass gives cover for a hunting weasel.

> Begone, Mr Newt,
> In your warty old suit;
> Come back, Mr Weasel,
> While I set up my easel.

Can this be Crispin returning betimes, presenting the appearance of a drowned rat? Methinks he forgot his jar of putty. Dear Crispin. His bubble-and-squeak is prepared to his liking.

I was just about to paint some ladybirds when I heard footsteps coming up the garden path. It was the master, with a scowling face. I ran downstairs to meet him, the bottle of milk clutched in my right hand like a cudgel.

'Come one step nearer and I'll brain you!' I threatened.

He ignored me completely and went to look in the oven. 'Isn't the dinner ready yet?' he inquired.

We passed a reasonably quiet evening, considering we were trying not to touch each other. It wasn't easy in that little Wendy house. 'Talking heads' again. With so many know-alls on the box, I don't know how the country's got into such a state. Litter strewn everywhere, dereliction, corruption, rape and pillage.

'If this is where freedom and democracy gets us,' said Otley, 'how about trying the Goths and Vandals for a change?'

An American film next, starring Meryl Streep, or was it one of the others with interchangeable names?

> Is Sissy Spacek Meryl Streep,
> Cloris Leachman or Stacey Keach?

It was a new Anglo-Saxon riddle I put myself to sleep with every night, having solved the one about the plough.

'Have you mended my socks yet?' came a plaintive cry.

I pretended not to hear and got on with my crossword puzzle. He then adopted a sterner tone of voice like Gladstone preaching to Queen Victoria. I looked the other way.

'Have you sewn the buttons on my blue-striped shirt?' he demanded.

'Clogs!' I snapped, as I put down my paper. He was only thinking of Bella. 'It's about time you learnt to sew your own buttons on.'

'Have you been out with that bloody Crispin again?'

If only Jeff were here! We could have an intellectual discussion about red dwarfs and parsecs, about white dwarfs and black holes, about super-novas and binaries; and he would wear silver socks that didn't want mending – only soldering, every light year or so.

I kissed him goodnight and left him looking for a red-triangle film on Channel Four. Never let the sun go down on your wrath Granny always told us. A Judas-kiss, Otley called it. I call it insurance.

MIKE CAME KNOCKING on the door the next morning when we were eating our boiled eggs and Marmite soldiers. Somebody had seen us fighting in the street and told him.

'Aren't you ashamed of yourselves?' he scolded.

'No,' said his father truculently. 'We've got as much right to be hooligans as you have.'

'You don't communicate any more,' Mike went on, 'reason things out.'

'It's the battle of the sexes,' I explained. 'That's all.'

'Sometimes you love 'em, sometimes you hate 'em,' added his father.

'You'll understand when you're married yourself,' I said.

'I'm not getting married,' Mike said, with a bit too much passion, I thought. I must remember to get those AIDS leaflets.

'It's not natural for men and women to live together, son. Animals part when they've mated, go their own separate ways; we're still together but it's not been easy.' Otley protested too much as a result of watching *Survival* for the third time round.

'We love each other really,' I said. I wanted Jeff now but didn't want to lose Otley and I knew that he wanted Bella and me as well. That must be love. I'm of sentimental value like an old bendy toy.

'There's the marriage guidance council,' Mike began.

'We don't need them,' I told him. 'Honestly we don't.'

'Sticking their noses into other people's business,' said Otley. 'Interfering gits.'

Well, Mike wanted to know, if we weren't going to the Canary Islands or the Dodecanese, would we go up to Shipley Glen on the Saturday with him and Heron? It was where we met, wasn't it? It would be like old times – take a picnic, have a ride on the Victorian tramway, get some snaps as it was our wedding anniversary.

'Oh! that will be nice!' I said.

'Can you lend me £50, then, I'm skint?' he said.

Otley fetched his Geiger counter to show Mike how it worked and they went clicking away through the nettles. Like father, unlike son. Mike tall with wild black hair, tight faded jeans and a hole in his white trainers, lithe as a jungle cat. Otley smart as a Godfather in white shirt, black pants and natty shoes, an old tom-cat out on the tiles. To be fair, he thinks I'm a fireside tabby, but I'm thinner now, more like an alley cat; and I musn't put any weight on if I'm going to get through one of those port-holes in the flying saucer – I couldn't see any other way in.

I cleaned up the kitchen and threw the recipe for *rogan josh* in the rubbish. You never see Mrs Chandra; she's always in the kitchen, stirring something in the cauldron. I can make a dock pudding, tie it up in support tights, put it in the old set-pot to boil away and Bob's your uncle! You can have a day out in Morecambe while it's doing.

I was longing to see my silver love so I went over to find

out if Thelma wanted any help. She was feeling better, wearing her safari suit, and carrying her rucksack and a voluminous black butterfly net. She strode out determinedly with the net over her shoulder like a rifle.

'Don't let that lot get in the kitchen and drink all the milk,' she was saying to Sylvie. She would try to get me a dragonfly but it was funny where the other one had got to; and she could swear there were some butterflies missing. Her sharp eyes flicked round the room and came back to rest on Sylvie.

'It's not me,' Sylvie cried. 'I haven't got them.'

'I didn't say you had,' said Thelma.

'You looked at me when you said it,' Sylvie replied fearfully.

'If the cap fits, wear it,' Thelma said, brushing her aside.

She sailed out like a brigantine to the strains of 'The Grand March' from *Aida* and Sylvie immediately turned the set off.

'I hope she gets run over by a steamroller one day,' she said.

'You don't mean that,' I said, for the sake of formality.

'Yes I do,' she went on. 'I want to see her squashed and pinned to a piece of cardboard like those poor little, innocent creatures.'

'Sylvie,' I said, pretending to be shocked.

'A great big pin right through her guts,' she said with passion.

I followed her into the kitchen where she opened the drawers of the heavy oak dresser and lifted out all the glass cases.

'Look at 'em poor little souls. What have they done to her?' she said.

There were butterflies from Peru, Persia and Kashmir; Corsica, China and Nepal; Borneo, Madagascar and Ilkley Moor. Flying jewels murdered in cold blood, their furry little corpses set out in neat rows.

'She puts them in the oven,' Sylvie explained. 'It's just like Belsen when she starts.'

I made some tea while she fetched Tinkerbell down for a fly round, first closing all the doors and windows. It was warm and humid, and I was fanning myself with the *Yorkshire Post* when Jeff came in.

'I saw you through the window,' he said, helping himself to some tea.

'Oh!' I said, giggling nervously.

'Where's the spear side?' It took me some time before realizing he meant Otley. He must have done geneaology at night-school as well.

'Out and about,' I told him. He could be anywhere by now. Jeff put his arm round me and I went dizzy for a second or two.

'He's a fool throwing you into somebody else's arms,' he said.

'Whose arms?' I asked, breathless.

'These,' he said, drawing me closer and looking into my eyes. I wanted to shut them and enjoy the sensation but I couldn't. I found myself watching a sort of video and didn't want to miss it – sort of *Dr Who* and *The Empire Strikes Back*, a spinning universe behind his electric gaze. When eventually we kissed it was like when I used to lick the bulb on my flash-light to see what it tasted like – salty and lemony with a red-hot tingle. I ran my fingers up and down his spine and there were no knobs on. His arms felt hard and shiny like lobsters' claws and I was held as if in a vice. It was a change from Otley and at my age I can afford to experiment. I have nothing to lose.

I don't know how long we stood there but suddenly it was as if the television had switched off and he was examining the butterflies, as if unaware of my existence.

'They're beautiful,' he said half to himself. 'We have nothing like that in . . .'

'In where?' I inquired.

'Oh! where I live in Catstones. It's bleak up there.'

'Why don't you move, then?' I asked.

'It's convenient for my work,' he said, not looking up. 'Nobody bothers me.'

'What work?' I said, like the Spanish Inquisition.

'I'm keeping a record of ancient rites and customs. Earth magic, we call it.' Did I see him take a specimen out of the case then? It looked like it but I couldn't be sure.

'Like morris dancing?'

'That's just a bit of fun,' he said. 'Oils the wheels, as it were.'

'What wheels?' I asked.

'I mean, keeps the motor running,' he said, winding his hand round.

'What motor?'

He straightened up and came over to where I was leaning, with my elbows over the table. His eyes silver-blue and shut off again.

'My motor,' he said slowly and distinctly as if talking to a retarded bandicoot.

'I only asked,' I said, moving quickly out of the way.

'Tinkie doesn't like Auntie Thelma,' Sylvie said, as she brought the birdcage into the kitchen. She opened the door to let him out and he perched on her head while she drank her tea.

'Anybody want a sandwich?' she inquired, bending down to get the bread out of a huge Ali Baba crockpot, the budgie swaying this way and that, legs spread out to keep his balance, like a drunken sailor on a rolling deck. She suddenly stood up and he rose into the air and settled down again in the same place.

'Jeff's on my side, aren't you, Jeff?' Sylvie said coyly.

'How d'you mean?' I asked.

'All that "oompah, oompah, stick it up your jumper" stuff; he doesn't know how I put up with it,' she said.

'That and brass bands – they give me earache,' he explained.

'It was lovely when she was out the other night, wasn't it, Jeff?' she said, picking a piece of cotton off his shirt, as if they were man and wife. 'We listened to all his favourites.'

'It's a long time since I heard them,' he said.

'What?' I was curious to know.

'Oh! *The Planets, Clair de lune* and that one they play on *The Sky at Night* – you know the one,' he said, in a trance.

'And that one that Frankie Vaughan used to sing, "Give me the Moonlight" and "When you You Wish Upon a Star" – all them oldies.' Sylvie smiled fondly at him and caught his hand in hers. Good gracious! She was in love with him. At her age! I'd better warn her – she doesn't know he's a tin man. I smiled at him too just to see if he smiled back and he did, he did. I don't suppose they care in outer space how many women they've got if they're five parsecs away from each one. Anyway my love is pure; we'll go whirling through the galaxy, gazing into each other's eyes, while Sylvie awaits his return with a brand-new Prestige can-opener.

When Jeff had eaten all the sandwiches and had gone to join the lads picking caterpillars off the cabbages, Sylvie fluttered through the house with a feather duster. I followed, straightening the antimacassars and knitted wool cushions that were piled up everywhere. She had in her time knitted so many squares for the Third World that they didn't want any more, so she sewed them into patchwork cushion-covers and blankets. Her great-grandmother on her mother's side was one of the demon knitters of Dent, world famous for their flashing needles.

'He's gorgeous, isn't he?' she said, pulling back the lace curtains in order to admire Jeff. He caught sight of her and waved.

'He's all right,' I said, not wanting to give anything away.

'I'm glad I've saved myself for him,' she went on, dropping the curtain and fleeing to the next window like a fugitive dryad. Her face was flushed and her blue eyes burned like the pilot-light on a multi-point gas heater.

We climbed the dark stairs and turned into a long passage with stained-glass windows too high to be opened: stylized tulips in red, blue and yellow; sailing ships and heraldic devices in forgotten golds and greens. The musty smell left by a century of heavy breathing and moth-balls caused us to choke.

'If we had a window cleaner we could get them open,' Sylvie said.

'Have you looked in the *Yellow Pages*?' I said, holding my nose.

'We've tried,' she said, 'but they all mark their own territory like dogs.'

'You can get extension ladders,' I said.

'They don't go that far up,' she replied.

'There's those magnetic things where you don't have to go outside,' I said helpfully. 'On the end of a long stick.'

'We've had one,' she sighed, 'and it's still stuck up there – half of it fell off.'

'What a shame,' I said sympathetically.

'We're going to have to set fire to it and let the fire brigade wash it down with their thingummyjigs,' she concluded.

We dusted down the ancestors before we left. Bearded men with stern looks and busty women with frizzled fringes; Queen Victoria's diamond jubilee and for some reason a portrait of Elizabeth, the virgin Queen, hung in an alcove.

'I hate her,' Sylvie said passionately. 'I wrote a poem about her once, when I was in bed with chicken pox.'

I looked closer at the piece of paper stuck on the wall by the side of the picture as in an art gallery. It was written in a childish scrawl, faded and with a smudge of jam across it:

Good Kween Bess in her pointy dress
All starchy ruffin is made of stuffin.

By me, Sylvie Brooks, High Riding, Yawkshire, Ingland, Yorrup, British Hempire, The World, The Yoonivers.

'What for?' I asked.

'She's like the wicked stepmother in *Cinderella*,' she went on. 'Jeff likes that spangly frock – he says it's like starlight.'

We dusted Mummy's room, all satin and lace and bows of pink ribbon. Nosegays and lavender bags and bowls of pot-pourri jostled with a glass menagerie and pots of African violets.

Then the master bedroom, mahogany and brass like the Captain's quarters on a man-o'-war. A leather-topped writing-desk and a pair of carved ivory book-ends holding *Wanderings in South America, Through the Brazilian Wilderness* and *A Pilgrimage to El-Medinah and Mecca*.

'She thinks she's a Big Daddy,' Sylvie said, giving them a token flick.

We paused to admire Jeff once more before I went home to do the dock pudding but there was a blank space where he had been a minute before.

'He keeps doing that,' Sylvie said. 'I don't know where he gets to.'

I was on my way through the wilderness when this bright light shot into the sky from the direction of the summer-house. Be like that, then, I thought – you might have given me a lift. The dock pudding gurgled away happily like a baby with no need of a nursemaid and for a while there was nothing to do.

10 July 2 AC
The sky Wedgwood-blue with little wisps of cloud like Johnson's cottonwool buds. My beloved compared it un-favourably to my eyes, composing me a madrigal on his

flute ere I awoke. He is to gather his flock to sing for the sheltered housing complex down Nelson Mandela Avenue. Brave Crispin. The lark sings on high, shooting up and down like a yo-yo, the river alive with dace and chub.

> Hail, friendly chubs,
> In your spotted frocks;
> I'm going to Woolworths
> For one of your locks.

'Tis my soul returned post-haste, stumbling blindly with a chamber-pot on his head; methinks the old folk fancy Bingo before 'Lead Kindly Light'. I will prepare a tisane of camomile for he surely hath a great headache. Noble creature! He trails a sack of kindling in his wake.

I was just stir-frying the dandelions when Otley came running down the crazy paving, his hair singed and his shirt in tatters.

'Did you see it?' he gasped, as soon as he could.

'Yes,' I said, lifting the green mess out on to a plate.

'I was coming down the beckside minding my own business when there was this whoosh of hot air; I threw myself down flat and it only just missed me,' he said, sinking into a squashy chair.

'D'you want chips with it?' I asked.

'It picked me up and flung me on to the boulders,' he said. 'I saw a grinning face at the window – I could swear it was that Jeff.'

That night I dreamt I was waltzing through the galaxy with Jeff in our very own starship. Our first interstellar home. We had just got back from our honeymoon on Epsilon Indi, where we stayed in this posh hotel, like the Grand Hotel at Eastbourne only it was made of plastic and there was no sea view, only a sky view – endless night, with stars like paper cut-outs stuck on a blackboard. In the morning we put our magnetic boots on to keep us stuck to the ground and went and sat on the promenade to watch the clouds come rolling in. Jeff did a tap dance and sang 'Wait Till the Sun Shines, Nellie'. It was turning out to be more of a soft-shoe shuffle so he took his boots off, forgetting where he was and went into orbit by mistake. Luckily, the *Starship Enterprise* brought him back and we retired thankfully to the bridal suite, a gigantic silver egg, where you could sit and look at each other all night; and if you looked hard enough you would get a little silver baby.

'Aren't you getting up today? We're supposed to be going to Shipley Glen.'

It was my Earthman waiting for his Marmite soldiers. What a rude awakening! I must confess I had slept heavily after my dock pudding and chips, but it would be nice to be kissed awake like Sleeping Beauty for a change. I can prick my finger and fall asleep all right but my handsome prince never comes.

'Your mother always said you were idle,' Otley grumbled, flinging the bedclothes on to the floor. 'All the other kids asked if they could stay up and you asked if you could go to bed.'

I leapt out of bed as I remembered. Me being the Mummy, I had to do a picnic for four, while he being the Daddy, he had to turn the place upside down looking for a clean shirt and socks. This was only the overture.

'Shall I put these pork pies in?' I asked, after clearing up the breakfast debris.

'No, I don't want salmonella poisoning,' said Otley.

'Tomatoes?' I queried.

'The pips get under my teeth,' he complained.

'This granary bread's nice,' I said hopefully.

'It's worse than the tomatoes.'

'There's a quiche from Marks & Spencer,' I tried next. 'Cheese and broccoli – your favourite.'

'You have to eat them within two days of purchase, haven't you? When did you get it?'

'Last week,' I said sadly, looking at the date.

'Throw it away, then,' he said, as if he were Paul Getty.

'I'll keep it for the ducks,' I said.

'Haven't you made anything?' He inquired in an aggrieved tone of voice.

'There's fried rice and prawn balls,' I said hesitantly.

'Are you trying to kill me?'

'I'll put this watercress in; I picked it wild the other day,' I said, proud at doing it myself.

'I don't want to get liver fluke, it comes down from the sheep on Bilberry Moor.'

'Why didn't you tell me then?' I said crossly. 'There'll be liver flukes all over the fridge now.'

'Oh! don't make such a fuss,' he said impatiently. 'Throw it all in a bag and I'll pick out what I want when we get there.'

It was chilly so I put on my jeans and a warm woollie over a long-sleeved blouse. Otley wore grey cotton cords, a grey shirt and a black nylon windcheater; he smoothed his disappearing coiffure down and ran his fingers over his chin. He was thinking of tomorrow when Bella would come back from Majorca with a bottle of duty-free and a pair of castanets.

'I'm only doing this for Mike's sake,' he gave me to understand.

'So am I,' I said, thinking of Jeff all alone in his silver egg.

Cohabiting with a *refusnik* is no joke and I am beginning to feel sorry for Mr Gorbachev.

We got off the bus by the almshouses at Saltaire and jostled up to the glen with the ethnic majority. Thank goodness Heron wasn't wearing his beads, just the normal tatty jeans like the rest of us. Down to the canal where a straggle of apparent fugitives were waiting to board the water-bus. Looking closer, I could see that they weren't refugees at all but ordinary mummies and daddies taking their little kiddiewinks to look at the Five Rise Lock. More 'refugees' waiting for the Victorian tramway so we tagged on at the end of the queue. You can walk up as quickly but that's not the point. We rattled our way up through the wood in an open-topped car with bunting flying, passing its twin brother coming down. We all laughed and waved at each other as if we were bound for New York in the *Queen Mary*. We got off at the top and bought some cinder toffee and a postcard of Sir Titus Salt at the souvenir shop. Mike took a snap of us holding hands and smiling at each other. We don't want to be blamed if he's had up for growing cannabis on his window-sill. He's not deprived – we've still got his Dinky toys up in the attic.

A panorama of moor and ancient woodland spread out before us, with the river Aire, the Leeds and Liverpool canal and the Settle–Carlisle railway jostling for position in the model village built by Sir Titus to rescue his army of worker ants from the sulphurous fumes of Bradford. They were just about to drive the Aire Valley trunk road through it when somebody remembered it was a conservation area.

'There's a stone circle somewhere here,' Heron told us. 'It makes a ley with Druid's Altar and the barrow on Thornton Moor.'

'Oh!' I said, 'That's interesting.'

'Going a bit north west,' he went on, 'and then going east over Kirkstall Abbey the other way on.'

'What's that mean?' Otley said, with his mouth full of cinder toffee.

'It's likely to be a power point,' said Heron.

We wandered around, bent double, looking for the magic circle but there were so many stones and boulders that we couldn't decide which was it. Somebody had hammered it into the ground.

'Let's have a break and we'll look for it after,' I said, sitting down exhausted by a flat rock that was just right for a picnic-table. I set out the various parcels and packets and everybody helped themselves. It was a bit smash-and-grab as we hadn't brought our own transport, unlike the people on the next rock with their posh basket, folding chairs, tablecloth and napkins, cutlery, including spoons for individual trifles from Marks & Spencer, and a coordinated tea-set and fruit bowls in red, go-anywhere plastic. They came in an Austin Princess.

Our fare was plain but honest: ham rolls, cheese-and-pickle sandwiches, a bag of lettuce and tomatoes to plunder at will, apples and home-made scones. We could call in somewhere for tea and sticky buns. I tried not to let our neighbour see me licking my fingers as she ran round with the baby wipes.

Mike and Heron seemed to be sharing a private joke, laughing at nothing and catching each other's eyes. I noticed Otley fidgeting and looking the other way. He surely didn't think they were . . . but Heron did seem a bit limp-wristed when I asked him to hand me something. I really must remember those AIDS leaflets. The government's supposed to have sent one to everybody but they might have missed Mike. He moves every few weeks into an identical bed-sit, barely a street away, and I have to go and scrub it out and clean the windows. On one occasion I washed the heavy velvet curtains; gave the chairs and carpet a beating in the backyard; papered the kitchen and lined the shelves in sunshine-yellow washable Contact; cleaned the windows and hung net curtains up; and then he moved. He needn't think I shall do it again.

Mike took a snap of us sharing an apple and nestling up to each other like turtle doves. Who says the camera can't lie? We resumed our search for the stone circle. Heron said that the earth was once peopled by giants from outer space and that Stonehenge was their astronomical clock. Somebody in America has found a thigh bone three feet long.

'It's spooky round here,' Mike said. 'Mind you don't get beamed up, Mum.'

The dark wood with its primeval crags lay in wait below and we planned to return that way later rather than take the tram. It was a pleasant walk following the beck and coming out on to the riverside.

'Anybody want a cup of tea?' inquired Otley.

We joined a crowd of what appeared to be shipwrecked mariners searching for buried treasure, which led eventually to the tea-rooms, and after much clashing of crockery and rattling of tin trays we found an outside table which we had to clear first before we could sit down. Otley went for a plate of Belgian buns and nearly got swept off his feet by a gang of lads and lasses on their way to the fairground singing their favourite song,

'Erewiggo, erewiggo, erewiggo! Erewiggo, erewiggo, erewiggo-o!'

Catching a glimpse of myself in a mirror and noting the general disarray of one and all after an afternoon on the rocks, I'm surprised they don't ban us all from Europe.

Otley picked all the currants out of his bun and arranged them round the edge of his plate.

'I wonder if there are any currants in space,' I said idly.

'You wouldn't be able to tell them from the black holes,' said Otley.

'What does it feel like to be reliving your youth,' Mike

asked, 'visiting your old haunts, retracing your footsteps, strolling down memory lane, experiencing that first consuming passion?'

'We come up here regular,' said Otley.

'Yes, but not together,' Mike pointed out.

'It's all right,' I said. 'Can't complain.'

I was bored stiff really but didn't want to hurt his feelings. It was nice of Mike and Heron to come with us but they should be out after crumpet. Two sirens brushed past us like ripe peaches in their tight pedal-pushers, earrings jangling and licking ice-cream cornets with lips like strawberry jam. Otley couldn't take his eyes off them but for the boys they didn't rate a second glance. I'm not going to get any posterity at this rate.

'They say the UFOs were active last night,' Heron said, finishing off his third bun. 'Like Blackpool illuminations, one chap told us.'

'Very nearly gave me a haircut,' Otley said. 'Did you see it?'

'When was that?' said Mike. Otley picked up his saucer as if to skim it.

'Early on, about tea time, there was this whoosh and it was gone.'

'Came in with his shirt in tatters,' I said. 'Not fit to be seen.'

'No,' Mike said, 'we didn't see that one.'

The tables in the tea-rooms were sliced out of tree-trunks that looked as if they had been struck by lightning with scorch marks from decades of cigarettes being stubbed out on them; ours even had a jagged end, as if a crocodile had snatched a bite. Otley moved up closer to me and brought his bun with him.

'I've just got rid of the currants; I don't want deathwatch beetle in it,' he complained.

We huddled together as the wind got up; it was almost a

second honeymoon. We poured each other's tea out and handed round nuts and raisins and bacon-flavoured crisps. Children and dogs ran rings around us as if weaving us into a cocoon. I didn't know how long this *glasnost* was going to last but it was getting to be suffocating.

'If we go back through the woods there's some yellow pimpernels, and some wild orchids in a field,' I said. 'I can put them in my diary.'

Otley jumped up suddenly and I was thrown to the ground as the bench tipped up. I collected my scattered belongings while everybody laughed as if it was a Charlie Chaplin film.

'You mustn't pick them,' Otley warned.

'I'm not going to pick them,' I said, 'I'm going to scrutinize them.' I had brought my spiral-bound, junior reporter's notebook.

'We'll go back on the tram, then,' Mike said. 'We've got some practising to do.'

Was that a secret signal meant for Heron?

'Hope it's helped you sort out your problems,' Mike continued. 'Lack of communication is the cause of much needless heartache.'

'Oh! I know,' I said.

'Man is born to trouble as the sparks fly upwards,' added Heron.

'Is he?' inquired Otley.

We waved our marriage-guidance counsellors off as they were absorbed into a straggling, dishevelled, multi-coloured stream of nature-lovers, heading for the tramway, an assortment of litter travelling in their wake.

'They should provide litter bins,' I said.

'We do,' said the girl who was clearing the tables, 'but they take them and leave the litter.'

'There should be government guidelines,' Otley observed. 'They've got guidelines for everything else.'

'Nobody takes any notice of them,' she said. 'You lay down guidelines on Friday and tell them it's a free country on Saturday – so they think they can do what they like.'

'And the dogs are a nuisance as well,' I said sympathetically.

'They shoot them in Peking,' she said.

'And ban them in Helsinki,' Otley added.

We made our way along the edge of the glen, stumbling over half-hidden boulders, any one of which could have been part of the stone circle. Coming the other way were the Ancient Britons, trying to find a path down through the wood. They went round in rings, looking baffled.

'I could have sworn it was here,' Daisy Rimmer said.

'Last time we came up the other way, we came out here by this tree,' Oggie said, 'so it should be here somewhere.'

They poked about in the undergrowth with their sticks, to no avail.

'It was over there by that big rock, wasn't it?' Doreen said.

'No,' Gilbert replied. 'I think we've passed it because wasn't there a caravan park right opposite at the top of the hill?'

It's one of life's mysteries that you can find the path up through Shipley Glen, but you can never find it down. The Ancient Britons went back the way they came and we slid down through the bracken till we were checked by a fallen tree lying across a track that led down to the beck.

'Mind how you go!' Their voices came down after us. Great black crags loomed among the trees like dinosaurs, and an old wych-elm hung at a crazy angle, its arms outstretched as if trying to get away from the menacing beasts. I squeezed through some mangled wire netting to look at the spotted orchids and sat down with my book.

'Don't be long. I want to get back in time for *Right to Reply*,' Otley called. 'I'll wait at the top.'

11 July 2 AC

Crispin has hied away to visit his old Nanny who is to have a hip replacement, taking with him a stick he has fashioned from our friendly apple tree. The sun hides behind a cloud, sad at his departing.

The purple orchis spreads her wings like a myriad flying angels, and the tall sweet cicely gives out her scent of aniseed balls. A robin is about his merry business.

> Robin-a-bobbin,
> Over the ground,
> It isn't Christmas
> All the year round.

My beloved returned, leaning wearily on his stick. Nanny has no use for it, giving up the ghost after waiting nigh on ten years for her operation. His sausages are sizzling on the wood-burning stove. He has remembered the HP sauce. Dear, thoughtful Crispin, he shall have the biggest egg.

The murky water of the old reservoir at Crag Hebble lay behind the trees like a slimy reptile. I stared, fascinated, when a golden glow suddenly lit up its surface. The trees bent as if in a hurricane and I moved closer on to the bridge to get a better look. The ground vibrated as if a hundred mad housewives had decided to vacuum the carpet at the same time. The bridge shuddered and then there was silence.

Was that a vehicle parked in the clearing? Funny place to leave a juggernaut. I crept towards it and after a beam of light had hit me I remembered nothing until I woke up and found myself clamped on to a table and saw a creature approaching with a hypodermic needle in his hand. I say hand but it was more like a claw. He had an eagle's head with feathers round his neck, kangaroo legs and a lion's trunk and tail, not unlike a griffin in a heraldic device. I tried to scream but no sound came out. The creature took a sample of blood from my left arm and then measured my head with a pair of callipers. He counted my fingers and toes, put the results into a computer and finally released me from the table. I stood up as he vanished from sight and I found I had regained my voice.

There was a star map of our solar system on the wall with little flags stuck on it which reminded me of War Games. In the centre of the room there was a transparent pillar with a column of light inside it that kept changing colour. On the wall opposite the map was a chart with names on it – Tunguska, Hiroshima, Nagasaki, Bikini, Windscale, Three Mile Island, Chernobyl. The fitments were all built into the fabric of the craft, folding up, sliding back or letting down as required. Food and drink dispensers, and a machine that looked like a one-arm bandit and a juke box combined were grouped together in a sort of space pub. I peered through the port-holes and could still see the trees. Thank goodness we weren't going anywhere. I hadn't brought my toothbrush.

The silence was eerie and I was beginning to suffer from sensory deprivation. They'd done all the tests and Otley would be waiting for me at the top of the field. If they let me know next time I can pack an overnight bag. I expected Jeff to appear or at least some sort of a silver man, but the griffin came back with something that looked like a dipstick. What was he going to do with that? He came towards me with his beady eyes and stopped about a foot away, his feathers ruffled.

'Do you speak English?' I said.

He ignored my question and prodded my ear with the dipstick.

'Steady on!' I shouted.

He jumped back, startled, entered something in the computer and advanced with a pair of scissors. Now what was he going to do? I shut my eyes and prayed. There wouldn't be time for 'The Lord's Prayer', so I said the one I wrote in my hymn book, next to 'For Those in Peril on the Sea', and inspired by the weather forecast,

> 'Rockall, Dogger, German Bight,
> Keep my Sole Fastnet tonight.'

He cut off a lock of hair and put it into a glass tube. I was tempted to pull out one of his feathers and make it into a quill pen like the ones Samuel Pepys used, but I had to get back to do the jacket potatoes and stir-fry sow-thistle. Pliny said it was good for the gravel.

In all this time my companion had not uttered a sound. He surely was not in charge of this Dr Who contraption. There must be somebody watching me through a two-way mirror.

'Take me to your leader,' I said, taking a deep breath.

To my amazement, I found myself sitting on the grass in the dark, clutching my bamboo pen minus its tassel. A ring of flattened grass told me I hadn't been dreaming and the surrounding bushes smelt like a burning compost heap. My wrist watch had stopped at five o'clock and I had no idea of the time. I ran and stumbled my way down to the river, over the bridge and on to the canal where I turned left at the lock. Walk ten steps; run ten steps; gasp for air; take a stone out of your shoe; walk ten steps and run ten steps up to the main road, where I sat on the wall by the bus shelter. Nobody stopped me and I could have been running away from Jack the Ripper for all they cared.

IT WAS MIDNIGHT when I got home, escorted by a full moon; although it was hidden at times behind the clouds, I was aware of its presence. Dogs barked, horses whinnied and cats caterwauled in back gardens. Angry voices accompanied slammed doors and babies cried in darkened bedrooms.

High Riding looked like a ship cast up on a reef, its chimneys like waiting vultures. Never fear, my Earthman is here. I picked up a big stone just in case. I could explain to the judge that I was building a rockery.

'Where the bloody hell have you been to?' the captain inquired.

'I was kidnapped by a flying saucer,' I said.

'You've been with that bloody Crispin again, haven't you?' Otley fumed. His eyes started swivelling and he picked up the Geiger counter as if he was going to throw it. He made a quick snatch at my notebook and riffled the pages.

'Trollop, bawdy-basket, cuckolder, doxy!' he spat.

I brandished my piece of millstone grit and went to meet him. 'Touch me,' I threatened, 'and I'll smash your face in!'

We faced up to each other with our weapons ready to bludgeon the other to death if necessary. He knocked the stone out of my hand and I brought my knee up to emasculate him, but he caught my ankle and flung me to the ground. I held on to his trouser belt as I fell and pulled him on top of me. We wrestled back and forth over the kitchen flags until I felt as if I had been under a stampede of wild mustangs. He reached his hand out for the roller-towel to strangle me with but I bit him before he could get to it. I had no more strength left so I decided to play possum. He'd be sorry I was dead.

'Are you all right?' he asked, as people do in the street when somebody's been run over. I didn't answer. Let him suffer.

'Where am I?' I asked, feigning ignorance and making a feeble attempt to rise.

'Thank God you're all right,' he said. 'I thought I'd killed you.'

'Water, water!' I gasped.

He threw a cupful in my face and I sat up spluttering.

'If you're all right now how about something to eat?' he asked.

'At this time of night?' I said. 'It's the witching hour.'

'It's time for the Hammer horror, then,' he said, switching on the box.

I was feeling a bit hungry myself so we had some cold dock pudding and a drink of milk, sitting there like two naughty children brought down for supper after being locked up in a darkened room all day.

'There's no need to lie to me,' he said. 'We're both grown up and these things happen; if you've got another bloke, say so.'

'I haven't,' I said.

'Oh yes you have,' he said.

'Haven't.'

'Have.'

'Haven't.'

'Have.'

'All right, then, I have,' I said.

'Why, you two-timing little bitch. I'll swing for you one day,' he swore, lunging at me and spilling his milk all over the put-u-up.

'We've abolished the death penalty,' I reminded him.

'You're the most aggravating little piece I've ever come across,' he said. 'No wonder I went mad.'

I mopped the milk up and made some tea. Christopher Lee was about to sink his fangs into a juicy neck, so I looked for the Mogadons in case Otley got ideas. The night was young.

'We'd better both have one or we'll never sleep,' I said.

'Who is he, then?' Otley inquired.

'Who?' I asked in surprise.

'This bloke you've got.'

'I haven't got a bloke,' I said.

'You just said you had.'

'I was mad at you,' I protested. 'That's why I said it.'

'What have you been doing all this time, then?' he demanded.

'I told you, I was kidnapped by a flying saucer,' I said. 'There was a thing inside with an eagle's head and kangaroos' feet.'

'And then what?' he asked.

'He took my measurements, looked in my ears and let me go,' I said, although I could hardly believe it myself. 'And he's got the tassel off my bamboo pen.'

'Have you got any witnesses?'

'No.'

'You realize this wouldn't stand up in a court of law,' Otley said.

'I'm not going in a court of law,' I said.

'No, but *I* might,' he replied with hidden menace.

I was too drowsy to argue about it so we watched the goings on in Dracula's castle in drugged togetherness.

'You know he came from Whitby, don't you?' Otley said, half awake.

'Who?' I mumbled.

'Dracula,' he said.

'That was Captain Cook,' I said. 'I've seen his house.'

'And Dracula,' Otley insisted.

'I didn't know he discovered New Zealand as well,' I said.

'Who?' said Otley.

'Dracula.'

'He didn't. That was Captain Cook,' he said with his eyes shut.

'You just said it was Dracula,' I said, but he didn't answer.

We fell asleep where we were, like the babes in the wood, and I had a good view of his black eye as my head came to rest on his shoulder.

A lot of people saw the UFO so Otley had to believe me in the end. Mrs Brackenbury was fetching the washing in when she saw it at the bottom of the street. She thought it was one of the new deregulated buses until it shot up into the air with a flash. Jimmy One Eye's cows ran amok when he was fetching them in for milking and he was trampled to death. The funeral was on the Thursday.

It was a damp, grey day just right for graveyards when we sneaked in to the back of the church, not knowing what to do as we are chapel. Ranged in the pews were fat, rosy little Mrs Brooklime, his widow, in an old black hat and coat that shone green like a beetle's wing. Dirk, his son, blond and rangy, awkward in a borrowed suit. Floradora, Mrs Brooklime's sister and Dirk's mother in black velvet, with shining jet and ostrich feathers in her large-brimmed hat, a relic of her theatrical days on the London stage.

Various aunts, all the uncles being dead, whispered into their handkerchiefs and sucked peppermint-creams; a waft of Parma violet and eucalyptus reached us from their direction. Old Ira Briggs from Whinclough Farm couldn't have long to go himself; had he come to gloat? Suddenly enemies had become friends, and folk who never had a good word to say to Jimmy when he was alive made pious faces now he was dead.

'Our brother James,' the vicar was saying, 'honourable son of the soil; pillar of the church; giver to charity; raiser of funds for the new hymn books; loving husband and father; friend of all and enemy of none.'

A rebellious muttering arose from some of the pews. They were here to bury Caesar not to praise him. Otley added his voice of dissent.

'Is it that ignorant git that stopped you going through his field they're talking about?' he said, nudging me in the ribs.

'Shhh!' I hissed, nudging him back.

'Well,' he said, 'bleedin' hypocrites.'

'I'll be blowed,' said one of the mourners behind us. 'You'd never recognize the mouldering old dungheap from that description.'

We saw him safely put away in the new cemetery as the old one was standing room only, then made our way like a flock of crows up the hillside for our ham tea and seed-cake. The sun was out after a damp start and the earth smelled like a steamy kitchen on wash-day. The grimy, mossy headstones of the ancients huddled together and frowned at us, as if they were saying, 'Look at them, they don't care about us'; and to be honest we didn't – they've had their day; this is ours. We would be joining them soon enough.

Scavenging hands cleared the table of bridge rolls, stuffing them into hungry maws as if feeding cement mixers. Mortal enemies hob-nobbed like long-lost cousins over the elderberry wine; false smiles drew out tit-bits of scandal to be relayed to outcasts forbidden to attend.

Miss Trickett, in her new bifocals, walked as if treading water and nibbled away at her seed-cake like a hamster. Floradora took advantage of a captive audience and sang 'Boiled Beef and Carrots' to cheer everybody up. Greg from London, in his cream corduroys and Aran sweater, stood out like a Charolais bull in a herd of black Aberdeen Angus.

'He's got a boutique down the King's Road,' said Mrs Brooklime.

Thank goodness Mike wasn't here.

All the goodwill had been used up by now and angry voices were heard coming from kitchen, bedrooms and hidden nooks and crannies.

From the alcove echoed, 'Before our Georgie died in 1960 he said I could have that walnut bedroom suite and you gave it to Aggie Jepson.'

'Well, she used to bandage his bad leg for him on a Friday.'

Down the stairs came, 'You never came to our Molly's funeral either.'

'I didn't know she was dead, we were at Aberystwyth.'

Drifting from the hall, 'I got nothing at all when Great Aunt Mildred passed away, only that stuffed sea-gull – you grabbed the lot.'

'I got the shock of my life when Pickford's van drew up and brought it all to our house,' answered an injured innocent.

'For two pins our Bert'll come round and flatten you!'

'You'll get a solicitor's letter if you talk to me like that!'

We didn't want to be involved in another punch-up so

we patted Mrs Brooklime on the back and left. How different it would be in space. A simple ceremony. A few galactic words. The press of a button. And you would be sprinkled into the blue like stardust.

'Wasn't that Jeff poking about in that field where they found the dead cow?' Otley said. My heart missed a beat.

'I didn't notice,' I said nonchalantly.

'I'll ask him when we go over tonight,' he said.

On the way back to High Riding we gathered ingredients for our hedgerow broth. Nettles, dandelion leaves, ground elder, fat hen – anything that looked likely, in fact. The broth always came out like hot swamp water, but it looked so nasty it was bound to be good for you. We never picked near the railway as it was rumoured that a train full of nuclear waste came through once a fortnight on its way to Sellafield. It's uneducated, ill-informed people like us that cause panic in the streets so we don't talk about it, in case it's just a vicious calumny. The government says we're in more danger from our television sets and holidays in Cornwall.

'Perhaps we are overdoing it,' I said. 'They seem to be getting back to normal in Chernobyl, hosing the streets down an' that.'

'They still haven't cleaned up Three Mile Island properly,' said Otley. 'As fast as they do it, they find the radiation's come out somewhere else.'

'And they're all right now in Japan,' I pointed out.

'If they're not dead, they are,' said Otley.

'Well, we're all right here if we're not dead.'

'There's more than one way of being dead.'

'How d'you mean?' I asked, digging up pignuts for our TV snack.

'Never you mind,' he said. 'And the next time a flying saucer gets you, dial 999.'

We got home in time for the news and I was enchanted

to learn that the FT Index was up 13.4, and the pound was unchanged against a basket of currencies. I looked in my purse but it was empty. Do they mean us? The High Street banks had lent billions to the Third World and would never get it back. That's what they call high finance.

'If I want to borrow a few quid to set up in business they won't lend me it,' Otley complained.

'I know,' I said sympathetically.

'You can only have it if you can prove you don't need it,' he said.

'Have a cup of tea,' I said, pouring it out.

'The bastards tried to charge me £2.50 for taking my money out of the Post Office and putting it in the bank,' Otley continued.

'It's daylight robbery,' I said.

'I wrote to the head office, complained to the manager, went through all the proper channels,' he said.

'What did they say?' I inquired.

'It was a routine charge and it had to stand. So I picked up a marble ashtray and threatened to brain the manager with it and they said they could cancel it, after all.'

'It's all helping the Third World,' I said. 'Mustn't be selfish.'

'Bugger the Third World,' he said.

'I thought we'd come up here to live like them,' I reminded him.

'That's to save my money, not theirs,' he explained.

He paced about while I made omelettes and chickweed salad, then dabbed his eye with witch-hazel. I thought he should get a pet to stroke. Something small and furry that didn't want much looking after. They're taking them into all the old folks' homes now; it stops them having heart attacks and nervous breakdowns.

'I'm off for a little aperitif,' he said. Bella was back!

16 July 2 AC

My love all day in the hills helping Farmer Ibbotson search for a lost sheep. He has been gone since cock-crow. Lack-a-day me! The setting sun tips the leaves with gold and it is time for the fairy cobblers to be about their task. I put out a dish of bread and milk for Bertie Badger. Sly old Reynard will get it first if we fail to apprehend him raiding the dust-bins.

> Poxy foxy,
> Jack-in-a-boxy,
> Caught in the bin
> With his head in a tin.

My bridegroom cometh over yonder knoll, leaning wearily on his shepherd's crook. Methinks he has been smitten with the scrapie as he halts to rub himself against a tree. I fain would make ready the sheep-dip ere he crosses the threshold. His dumplings are done. Dear Crispin.

I painted some feathers and ladybirds, had a watering-can shower and went down to watch the television. Like Pandora's box, once it's opened the world's ills come rushing out at you. It's not my fault half the world is starving to death and the other half is murdering each other. I'm sat here minding my own business. I've got enough to cope with as it is. I began to think longingly of the blue yonder, just me and my silver love and the infinity of star-spangled space. I can always come back on an away-day to make sure they were all right down below.

The door burst open and Otley came in, carrying two white rats in a cage. The musty smell came nearer and I looked into four pink eyes.

'This is Mickey and Minnie,' he said. 'A bloke gave me them.'

If Porsches are what the Yuppies acquire, then rats are what the Downwardly Mobile Old Nerds get.

'You said get something small and furry,' Otley reminded me, in an offended tone of voice. 'They won't eat much.'

'Their tails aren't furry,' I complained. And he was wrong about them not eating; they ate everything they could get their teeth into: books, newspapers, jumpers, footwear and furniture – and that was just in-between-meal snacks.

Minnie liked to run up your trouser legs and Mickey took a fancy to sitting on Otley's head when he was watching television.

'Leave him,' he said. 'It might make my hair grow.'

In the next few days I spent a lot of time in the big house helping out. I didn't want to tell him to get rid of his new toys in case he went and jumped off Stoodley Pike. Share his interests when he had a funny turn, the doctor said, or he'd feel rejected and unloved. I even went fishing with him once but I got the hook caught in his pants when I was practising, and we had to travel all the way home with him on the end of the line. He was very cross and wouldn't speak to me. So I went to Bridlington for a week.

He said when he was fed up with Mickey and Minnie they could go in the flying saucer in the cause of science, while we learnt how to drive. If a monkey can drive a starship we should be able to.

He sent me down to the market for some rat food and to the library to see if there was a handbook called *Understanding Your Rat*. I was going to Sammy Chandra's as well but Otley didn't want to bother coming with me. He was fed up with being told he was on the cusp.

'Don't be late back – we've got dancing practice after tea,' he said.

'I won't, I won't,' I promised.

'And no hanky-panky,' he warned.

'How d'you mean?' I said, making out I didn't understand.

It was airless and humid with a sky the colour of dirty washing-up water. A grey murk came down from the hills and wrapped me in cling-film. Was this the greenhouse effect they kept telling us about? I intended to throw away my lemon-scented aerosols the minute I got back home. Ancient stone houses dotted the hillside like grazing sheep, their little gardens splashed red with geraniums and blue with meadow cranesbill. These gave way to newer pebble-dashed ones with runner beans and rambler roses; and sometimes a dark, begrimed terrace where the sun never shines and nothing grows but moss and ferns. A town centre like a mad Catherine wheel.

It was children's story-telling in the library and a pub poet was acting out his own work, alternately jumping in the air and flinging himself on the floor. I found a book about rats and mice and one for myself about how to cook a square meal at fifty pence a head. There was a long queue waiting to come out as the computer had broken down again.

'Did you hear about that woman who was kidnapped by a flying saucer the other day?' the reader in front said to her companion.

'No, I didn't. When was that?' she asked.

'About a week back now. Took her up to Mars, had their way with her and threw her out again.'

'They didn't!'

'Found her wandering in a daze on Bradford Road.'

'It's not safe to go out, is it?'

'Her husband was furious,' the first one said.

'I should think he was,' her friend tutted. 'How did they . . .?'

'How did they what?'

'Well, you know, how did they have carnival knowledge?'

'With a dipstick, she says.'

It seemed a pity to come into town just for rat food, so I went round the shops to see what I would buy if I had the money.

There was a three-piece suite in coral chintz, with white peonies and blue birds of paradise. It broke my heart to look at it.

I pressed my nose up against the jeweller's window where there was a star sapphire like Princess Di's engagement ring. I might be able to afford the imitation one in Ali's Bazaar down Navigation Street.

A tweed costume in the Co-op, but even they were getting too posh for us Downies. There might be something akin to it in Oxfam.

A hand-made futon would be nice for Mike in his little bed-sit. He could fold it up and steal away like a bedouin when he's ready to move on.

A Montego Turbo in *Moonraker* blue for Otley and he could think he was in his own very own *Starship Enterprise*.

A last look at all the cream cakes, custard pies, curd tarts and chocolate eclairs that I'm trying not to eat because they're bad for you, and it was time to go and see Sammy Chandra.

'What occurred to Mr Brooklime is a calamity of the first degree,' he declared, inserting a betel leaf under his tongue.

'It was bad luck, that's for sure,' I said.

'It was karma,' he said. 'Mr Brooklime's just desserts for persistently chastising the sacred beasts.'

'How's the family?' I inquired, picturing the brightly coloured birds of paradise perching on their favourite branches of the family tree, preening their feathers and rising to catch a tit-bit thrown by their delighted owner.

'Saraswati has a touch of rheumatism,' he said. 'Amba is taking judo instruction and Sita has moved into a council flat; I don't know what is to become of us.'

'And Mrs Chandra?' I asked out of politeness.

His face turned into a thunderstorm, his eyes like flashes of forked lightning.

'Do not even mention her name,' he said.

'I won't,' I said, anxious to please.

'She is consorting with a ticket-collector on the Hallam Line,' he intoned in his beautiful English, 'and obtains free travel all the way to Sheffield.'

'Will you be getting a divorce, then?' I asked foolishly.

'A divorce? No,' he said, and suddenly a knife appeared in his hand. 'I will cut her in little pieces and distribute her along the track.'

'Oh! dear, don't do that,' I said.

'I shall report her to the authorities first,' he added. 'I am a law-abiding citizen.'

'Well,' I said, standing up, 'I'll be on my way. I've got to get the dinner ready.'

'Your stars are the same as last week,' he said, glancing at the charts. 'You are going on a long journey.'

'And the consternation?' I asked.

'It is still there.'

He showed me to the door, the eyes of the famous looking down from the walls in scorn; his shoulders bowed, defeated, humiliated: an astrologer who couldn't manage his own karma. Then suddenly his face brightened. The astrologer might be defeated but the businessman was not. He fetched out a tray of sweetmeats: pink rounds, green squares, red diamonds, gold nuggets and white coconut triangles amid an aroma of almond, nutmeg, cinnamon and aniseed.

'Perhaps you would like to purchase some *halva*, or *jalebi*?' he said.

I bought the green, almond-scented squares and put them in my handbag with the rat food.

'Next week we will be experimenting with red squares and green diamonds, and the coconut triangles will be produced in pink,' he explained.

'Oo! that'll be nice,' I said.

All this passion was giving me a headache. I would need a lie down when I got home. Aspirins and a cup of tea. Anoint my brow with Hungary Water. Close my eyes and think of black holes.

Otley was testing the rhubarb for milliSieverts before I stewed it with some dates. I looked in my library book and found a recipe for pauper's pottage. You get a big pot and put in odds and ends of anything you can find and boil it until it congeals. You do that every day, keep throwing things in and it can last all week.

'How's Mike, then?' Otley wanted to know.

'I forgot to pop in,' I said. 'I expect he's all right.'

'That Heron,' he said, 'd'you think he's . . .?'

'Think he's what?' I prompted.

'Well – d'you think he's bifocal?'

'I'm going to get some AIDS leaflets just in case,' I said.

'Did you see that thing on television where Norman Fowler's head came right up to you and said CONDOM?' Otley enquired.

'They've got to do something, haven't they?' I said. It was just one more worry come out of Pandora's Box. Becquerels, unemployment, strikes, football hooligans, E numbers. Where would it all end?

'It's a worry,' I said. 'I want some posterity to leave my diary to; we'll have to register Mike with a sperm bank.'

'Lawrence of Arabia did all right for himself,' said Otley.

All the same, I made a mental note to look for the signs next time I went down home: Nazi uniforms, Oscar Wilde, Starsky and Hutch.

'I wonder if there are any in the *Yellow Pages*,' I mused.

'What?'

'Sperm banks.'

'What category d'you think they'd come under, then?' Otley jeered.

I hadn't really thought. Bloodstock Agencies, Bridal Requirements? Or perhaps under one of the more mysterious headings like Flow Control Equipment or Profile Cutting.

'I don't know,' I confessed. 'We might have to contact Mr Steptoe.'

'That lecherous old git. What's he got to do with it?' said Otley.

'I mean the eminent professor who supervises test-tube babies,' I said. 'He keeps them in jars like tadpoles.'

'We only want one or two posterity,' he said. 'We don't want a bus queue.'

We had fungus on toast and sautéd sow-thistle, with rhubarb and custard, and green squares for pudding. Then, when I had cleaned up the kitchen, Otley let Mickey and Minnie out to mess it all up again. I went upstairs to lie down in case they wanted to sit on my head as well.

That night the UFOs came over again from Hebden Bridge way; they seemed to stop over the reservoir, make a falling-leaf manoeuvre and shoot off at right angles towards the north. It was just at the time of day when you're not sure whether you've seen something or not – the half-light when bats flitter and you think it's something in your eye.

We had gone over to High Riding and suddenly Jeff ran outside. He knew they were there before we saw them. He ran down to the summer house shouting and waving and we followed him. I could have sworn one of them dropped something and he picked it up, but when we asked what it was he said, 'Nothing.'

He seemed to be all lit up from inside like a neon sign, and every time I went near him it seemed as if an electric current passed between us. But first we had to do some dancing: 'Swaggering Boney' in which the morris men went leapfrogging all over the place, 'The Nutting Girl' and then 'Young Collins' again because of the tricky sticks.

'You've gotta be stick-perfect for the bank holiday,' Jeff told the men.

Finally they did 'Mrs Casey' again, with the clap behind the head.

'Not the earoles. Not the earoles,' Jeff kept reminding them.

I wondered what sort of earoles they had in space. The silver man up at Broadhead's farm had pointed ones like Mr Spock; I couldn't see the griffin's for his feathers; and Jeff's seemed to be just like anybody else's. Perhaps he was an android.

Thelma put the television on to see Charlton Heston in *The Ten Commandments* and Sylvie rushed out screaming.

'I'm not watching that Big Daddy with his beard and his tablets.'

'Shut your gob!' Thelma called after her.

Otley went to the Rose & Crown and the lads vanished one by one as the evening wore on. I stayed for a while and then, as I'd seen *The Ten Commandments* umpty times before, I went for a wander round the garden.

It was a clear night with the last sliver of the old moon lying like a cutting from God's toenails. All the flowers appeared white, except the red ones which had turned black. I picked a cabbage-rose to paint for my diary when I got back home. Home, where the rats live! I was beginning to dread going home. Little holes nibbled in everything. One day I had found several baby rats nestling in the eiderdown. I didn't know whether to scream or to be glad I was a grandmother. The next day they had gone – their mummy had eaten them for breakfast! It's like a video nasty. If he doesn't get rid of them I shall leave him.

I've promised to look after them tomorrow while he goes fishing. Just this once, he begged. He looked so worried and forlorn that I didn't like to say no, in case he had one of his funny turns. What can you do? It's always my fault: I'm not sympathetic; I don't make any attempt to share his interests. There was the time I used to run home from work to attend car-maintenance classes with him, and I was so tired that I fell asleep half-way through. Then, when I asked him to go to dancing classes with me, he said was I trying to make him into a ponce. If I'd have had a funny turn it would have been my own fault.

I'm ready to go into orbit any day. I kept the rose up to my face so that the scent would drown the smell of the rats. I'd let him have his day fishing then give him an ultimatum: it's me or them.

'I thought I'd find you here,' Jeff said, jumping out from a bush.

'Oh! you startled me,' I said in a poor imitation of a heroine in a romantic novel.

'It's a lovely night,' he replied, scanning the firmament with his silver-blue eyes.

'Has the film finished?' I asked, for no reason.

'I've seen it before,' he said.

'Haven't we all?' I laughed.

We walked close together, there was no need to touch as a magnetic field seemed to be all around us, more vibrant than physical contact.

'This is yours, I believe,' he said, holding his hand out towards me.

It was the tassel off my bamboo pen. How had he come by it?

'You dropped it in the skimmer the other day,' he said.

'Skimmer, is that what it is?' I asked.

'Earthskimmers are based on the Moon; Recorder Five is engaged in collecting samples and . . .'

'Was I a sample?' I interrupted hastily.

'Of course,' he explained. 'It is all in the interests of scientific research.'

'If you had asked me I'd have given you my measurements,' I said.

'The Kraaks have their orders and must carry out their tasks,' he replied, picking a carnation and inhaling its spicy perfume.

'What do you do with all the samples?'

'We are growing them in the botanic gardens; we have nothing as beautiful as Earth flora,' he said wistfully.

'Where is your home?' I asked him.

'I live on the Moon. We came in a generation starship from Eridani. The old ones ventured out on a voyage of discovery; children were born, grew old in their turn and died on the long journey. We of a later generation reached the Moon and built our colony there.'

'But why did they leave in the first place?' I asked.

'Our planet was poisoned and could no longer sustain life,' he said. 'We are afraid the same may happen to Earth.'

'That would be a shame,' I said.

'It's nice down here,' he said, 'if it wasn't so dirty – litter everywhere, nuclear waste dumps, chemical pollution, dog mess.'

'I know,' I said.

'All this water as well. There's no water on the Moon.'

'How d'you go on for bathing?' I asked.

'We have a dry clean,' he said, 'and we go to the irrigation plant on special occasions; I miss the shower when I'm back there.'

'One thing that puzzles me . . .' I began hesitantly.

'What's that?' he said, sniffing at the carnation.

'Why do you go sneaking about your business like you do? If you're worried about what we're doing down here, why don't you come out into the open and say so? Go on *World in Action* or *Panorama* an' that.'

'You must be joking!' he said. 'You're like a pack of ravenous wolves. Look at all the bloodshed – you're still barbarians.'

'It's not so bad in Keighley,' I said.

'You haven't learned how to live with each other yet, never mind Martians or Moonmen; we'd get torn to pieces.'

'It's not as bad as all that,' I said. 'Everybody's not the same.'

'It's worse,' he said.

'Next time you go up there I'll come as well,' I volunteered.

'That'll be nice,' he agreed. 'We can watch the Earth rise.'

'I'm only coming for the day,' I told him. 'I like to sleep in my own bed.' He said it was all right and I needn't bother packing.

I WAS SO excited that I couldn't sleep that night. I even forgot to write up my diary. What did he mean, 'Don't bother to pack'? I hope it's not a nudist colony they've got on the Moon. It looks a bit chilly up there. Perhaps he's had a silver boiler suit specially made for me. That would be why they wanted my measurements. They didn't ask what size shoes I take, for my magnetic boots. I'll have to take my wellies and fill them with sand. Neil Armstrong went jumping about all over the place like a jack-in-the-box. I don't want to go over the edge.

I'm looking forward to seeing the botanic gardens. I went on a picnic to Kew once to see the giant water-lilies. But it was shut. We went to Battersea Park instead. I hope the Moon's not shut. I wonder if they've got any souvenir shops. I shall have to bring them a present back. A door-stop made out of Moon rock. Shaving mug with 'A Present from Mare Tranquillitatis'. A postcard with a view of the Leibnitz and Doerfels Mountains. A stick of rock with

Longomontanus all the way through. A piece of skyweed to hang up for telling the weather with.

I'd be interviewed on the *Nine O'Clock News* – 'How does it feel?' they'd say. Appear on the *Dame Edna Everage Experience*. Maybe even get a *Blue Peter* pencil. The night passed quickly in Moon-dreams and it was dawn before you could say flying saucer.

'Aren't you getting up today?' the master called.

'I'll be down in a minute,' I answered, with a barefaced lie. I managed to snatch forty winks before he shouted again.

'You know I'm going fishing today, don't you?' he reminded me.

'I'm coming,' I said sleepily. I tried to open my eyes but I couldn't. I dreamt I was up and doing the sandwiches. Potted meat, cheese and pickles, tomatoes, individual fruit pies, slab cake. I went to wave him off. 'Don't be late for dinner,' I said. 'It's Moghlai chicken braised with almonds and raisins, potatoes cooked with ginger, Mysore spinach with dill and jam roly-poly'.

'Tea up,' he shouted in my ear. 'Have you broken a leg or something?'

'Are you back already?' I said, stretching myself under the blanket.

'I haven't gone yet,' he said. 'I haven't got my sandwiches.'

'I just gave you them,' I mumbled.

'Are you all right?' he asked. 'Or do you want a doctor?'

'I want a doctor,' I said, to see what he'd say.

'There's nothing wrong with you – it's just lazyitis,' he said.

'Why did you ask if I wanted a doctor, then?' I challenged.

'Just to see what you'd say,' he said.

He was losing weight on our do-it-yourself diet, which

gave him a sharper look, a quicker step and the old jauntiness in his walk. Whether it was Bella or the flying saucers I don't know, both I expect, but it was a relief to find him getting back to normal. Though the ball-bearings still rattled round in his head from time to time. Poor love! He can't help being nasty. It's his molecules.

'Don't forget to give Mickey and Minnie a run round when you clean the cage out,' he instructed, as I did the sandwiches.

I had done baby-sitting but never rat-sitting. 'I daren't touch them,' I said, with a shudder. 'I don't like their tails.'

'You said you would.' He looked bereft. 'You promised.'

'Just this once, then.' I always try not to break a promise. 'But what if they won't go back in the cage?'

'Just leave the door open and they'll go in when they're ready,' he said, striding off through the nettles and cabbages.

'When they're ready!' he said. Not when *I'm* ready. I'm not putting up with this much longer. I'd stay on the Moon for good but what about Mike? Supposing he has a meaningful relationship with Heron and they set up house together in San Francisco. I don't want everybody saying, 'It's his mother's fault; she's gone to the Moon', I really will have to apply for sheltered housing accommodation. They only have to pay five pence for their television licence.

I got the pottage bubbling on a low light, added an onion and a sprig or two of goutweed – it being good for the 'jointe-ache' – and left it to its own devices.

I shut my eyes and opened the door of the cage and eight little feet scurried over my shoes. I put clean straw in and filled up the water dish, made some coffee and sat down with a crossword puzzle. It was difficult to concentrate with nibblings and gnawings going on all around me. I spread out some old newspapers, which was a mistake as it only emphasized the pattering of tiny feet. I tried to ignore them but when they chased each other up my legs and over my shoulders it was getting a bit much. Then Mickey ran up my back and sat on my head, while Minnie examined my ears. I screamed and shook them away and they scuttled off into a dark corner, mightily offended. Scurry under the dresser; scamper over the chairs; skitter under the put-u-up and round the skirting board; make some confetti; eat a geranium; run off with a wallflower; pitter-patter, helter-skelter, what fun!

I know I promised for better or worse, till death us do part. But it didn't say anything about rats or I wouldn't have signed up. I helped Minnie into the cage with my foot but Mickey was nowhere to be seen. I detected scratchings coming from inside the put-u-up and tipped it upside down. There was a little hole in the upholstery and two beady little eyes looked out at me.

'Come on, Mickey,' I said, holding out a piece of apple. 'Good boy, Minnie's gone back in the cage.'

He didn't seem to know what I was talking about and I followed the fortunes of a lump proceeding about its business inside the settee for an hour or more. I didn't want the woodwork to be eaten and the next do-it-yourselfers mutilated when they got into bed.

Breaking point came when I caught hold of his tail as it came past the hole and he bit me. I locked Minnie up and went out for a walk. I've kept my word; now it's me or them.

It was a warm sunny day so I went up on to the moors to pick some bilberries. Enough to make a flat pie would be all I would have time to get as I wanted to catch up on my diary. I made a nest in a patch of bilberries and sat there until I had stripped everything within reach. Did they have bilberries on the Moon? Moonberry pies an' that.

25 July 2 AC

My love is over the hills and far away, bringing comfort to

the worried mother of a football hooligan. He is wearing his Manchester United scarf to show his solidarity with the masses.

The waters of Ponden lie sparkling below like the Blue Lagoon. A red sailing dinghy skims the surface like a gaudy butterfly, until a NATO jet roars over and the sailors topple into the drink. A grouse rises up from the heather as I pass by.

> Poor old grouse,
> Fat as a louse,
> Off to the table
> In Grosvenor House.

I grow weary waiting for my beloved; but see, he comes! He enters, gasping for breath, his scarf knotted tightly about his neck. Our friendly, neighbourhood football hooligan is a supporter of Manchester City.

Fret not, dear heart, I will prepare your Rumbledethump ere you disentangle from your bondage. I fear you didst forget the kindling. Go back for it after supper.

I took the long way back, reluctant to return to my rat-infested hovel, seeing what I could find that I could make use of in the hedgerows and fields. Corn mint to put between cheeses to keep them fresh; now I only wanted the cheeses. Tansy to make a pudding with as a change from dock. Wormwood to keep the flies away. Feverfew for my headache, which I am sure to get. I sat down by the beck to pick a stone out of my shoe when I noticed a young man behaving in an odd sort of way. He was carrying a holdall and he seemed to be glancing around furtively to see if anybody was watching him.

What was he up to? Disposing of a body? Was it Mrs Chandra? Had Sammy changed his mind about scattering her along the railway line and hired a hit man? He didn't look like an Indian, though. Perhaps it was the IRA hiding a cache of explosives. Or the Arab Fundamentalists. Then again it might be the Basque Separatists. Or the Tamil Tigers. The Contras. The PLO. Plaid Cymru. Greenpeace. Red Brigade. Mafia.

I hid behind a bush when he put the holdall down and unzipped it. He thrust his hand into it and extracted a python, which he placed on the grass. I froze with terror when it came towards me. I wanted to run but couldn't.

'Take it away!' I yelled.

He looked startled and then made a dive for it, winding it round his arms as if it were knitting wool.

'I didn't see you there,' he said apologetically.

He seemed like a decent chap. Spanking clean, shirt well-ironed, new Levis; honest brown eyes, shining nut-brown hair and a ready smile. Nothing about him to indicate that he might be a snake charmer.

'You frightened me to death,' I said. 'Is it yours?'

'I've got to bring him down here every day for a slither,' he said.

'Where d'you live?' I asked, making a mental note not to go round that way.

'In the council flats,' he said. 'They'd evict us if they knew – you're not allowed to keep pets; but we came from Serpentis.'

'Where do you put him?' I inquired, trying to hide my revulsion.

'He sleeps by the boiler – he likes his home comforts,' he said, deftly moving his head this way and that to avoid the serpent's flicking tongue.

'Careful, he's going to bite,' I said, stepping back fearfully.

'He's only playing,' he said fondly. 'He's very affectionate.'

'What's his name?' I asked, expecting it to be Rajah or such like.

'Gordon,' he said, 'and I'm Steve Hurst.'

I gathered my things together to leave the field clear for Gordon but he said they were going home. It was time for his feed and it would have to be a dead rabbit.

'I bring him out for exercise; the neighbours complain when he goes in the garden,' he explained, 'and he catches some fresh food – it's better for him.'

'Live ones!' I shuddered, thinking of various missing cats and dogs.

'Rats and mice, water-voles, things like that,' he said, pushing the snake back into the holdall. He zipped it up and I felt I could breathe again.

Rats, he said. What luck! I could tell Otley I'd found them a good home; but if I did it behind his back he might go looking for them. I'll wait till he gets back tonight.

'I've got a couple of rats you can have,' I told him.

'Oh! thanks, that's great,' he said. 'I'll pay for them, of course.'

'It doesn't matter – we had them given. If you can call up at High Riding tomorrow you can have them – and the cage,' I promised.

'Thanks a lot,' he said, and his wholesome countenance shone at the prospect of providing his pet with a blood sacrifice.

'Ask at the cottage for Mrs Craven,' I called, as he went on his way with his wriggling holdall. 'And don't bring Gordon, will you?'

There's nowt so queer as folk. I thought, as I watched him until he disappeared behind the signal-box on the shutdown railway line. If they've got snakes on the Moon, I'm not going.

When I got home Mickey was sitting on top of the cage waiting to go in, as if butter wouldn't melt in his mouth. Minnie was looking up through the bars anxiously at him as if to say, 'It's not my fault, she shut the door.' He'd had a whale of a time. Flowers pulled out of their vases with half-eaten stalks littered the floor. I opened the cage door and helped Mickey in with a broom handle. Then I made some tea and sat down to do a crossword. It would have to be pauper's pottage tonight as I didn't feel like cooking. I wasn't hungry.

Otley was late and I didn't know when to expect him. He could be all night fishing for all I knew, and I was sick to death of the gnawing and scrabbling and squeaking going on behind me. So I threw a piece of old carpet over the cage and went out for some fresh air.

Walking in a temper, I went further than I'd intended and found myself on the way home through Low Riding. I decided I might as well call in and see Mike now. Make sure he wasn't up to anything. They were up to having a disco and red, green, blue and gold lights lit up the garden like a firework display. I had to lip-read through all the noise. No, he didn't want any washing doing. Yes, they'd clean up after it. No, they weren't smoking a joint; that funny smell was air-freshener. Yes, they'd lock up and no, they wouldn't set the place on fire. Dirk Brooklime and Susan Mitchell were bobbing up and down like on *Top of the Pops*, and a ghastly noise was blasting from a cassette player.

'It's our new number, "Silver Riding". What d'you think?' Mike asked.

'It's lovely,' I lied. I went upstairs to check the bedrooms. No cases packed, no passports or tickets to San Francisco. Maybe they'd hidden them in the attic. I went up to check. You've got to be one jump ahead. Everything seemed to be in order. Old copies of *Private Eye*, Davy Crockett hat, piles of hit singles, Scrabble and Monopoly, Dinky toys, cowboy outfit and a pistol that looked real enough to frighten anybody in the dark. I slipped it into my handbag as I had to walk home alone.

'Oh! Mrs Craven, there is a dreadful cacophony issuing from your house this night,' said Sammy Chandra, when I met him outside. His eyes seemed like burning opals in the changing lights. I could only apologize and inquire after his health. The wheel of fortune had turned again.

'Mrs Chandra is cooking the onion *bhajis*; I have agreed to take her back. Her paramour is transferred to the Minster and Selby line.'

'Oh! good,' I said. 'I am pleased.'

'These bloody ticket-wallahs are not to be trusted, patrolling the train as if it is their own property,' he said, his moustachios bristling.

'I know,' I said.

'Punching holes everywhere, when they have already been punched.'

I walked back slowly up the hill to High Riding, which was lit up by a golden glow. A large, dark shape hovered over the summerhouse. The light switched to blue, then red and white before shooting off in a westerly direction. Was it the Earthskimmer? Had I missed it?

When I got in, Otley and Mickey and Minnie were waiting impatiently. Where had I been to? I was supposed to be rat-sitting. I promised.

'I've just about had enough of those blessed rats,' I exploded. 'I couldn't get Mickey back in the cage; he's been inside the put-u-up all day – mind it doesn't collapse when you get in it.'

'Just pick 'em up by the tails and put 'em back,' he said.

'I tried but he bit me. Look,' I said, showing him my finger with the sticking-plaster on. 'He's been eating all the flowers.'

'They like flowers,' he explained.

'Look,' I said, 'it's either them or me. I want them out of here tonight.' He seemed to ignore me and looked in the oven for his dinner.

'It's on the top,' I said, pointing to the pottage mouldering away.

'Is that all?' he inquired, crestfallen.

'I had to get out,' I said. 'I couldn't stand it any longer. Why didn't you get a gerbil or something?'

He put his arm round me as if he were helping an old lady across the road. I'd feel better in the morning. I was overwrought. Would I like one of his Mogadons? Everybody wanted gerbils. Nobody wanted rats. He couldn't abandon them, unloved, unwanted. What would they do?

I wrenched myself away. It was now or never. I picked up the cage. 'They're going outside. It's me or them – make up your mind,' I said.

'And supposing I say them?' he queried, with a wicked grin.

'Why don't you give them to Bella to look after?' I yelled.

We struggled in the doorway as he tried to get the cage back. The rats ran backwards and forwards in a frenzy. I was getting hysterical. He was determined to get his own way as always. He snatched the cage and put it back in its corner. He pushed me violently as I reached for it.

'I'll get them a wheel,' he said. 'They needn't come out.'

'I don't like them; they smell,' I screamed at him, 'and I don't like their tails.'

'Oh! go to bed,' he said crossly.

I went upstairs, sobbing, and threw myself on the bed. Then I felt the gun in my handbag as I hung it on the brass bedknob. I washed in the big jug and basin and began to feel better. I took the gun and crept down again. He was watching *Murder, Mystery, Suspense* on ITV.

I pretended to be going to make some tea, crept round the back of him and stuck the gun in his ribs.

'Put 'em up,' I snapped.

'What the devil . . .?' he began, his face draining white.

'Are you getting rid of them bloody rats or not?' I demanded.

'Well, if you feel like that about it,' he said, picking them up and strolling casually to the door. I followed him with the gun.

'And get a move on,' I said, 'or I'll let you have it.'

'I KNEW IT wasn't a real gun,' Otley said, the next morning, as we ate our coddled eggs and our chemical-free Crackly Crunch.

'The principle's the same,' I said. 'I'd have murdered you if it had been.'

'I know,' he said.

'People have killed for less,' I added.

'Are these eggs Danish?' he enquired.

'I don't know,' I said. 'I never looked at the box.'

'They taste fishy,' he said, pushing it to one side. 'They use up all the spare herrings for chickfeed.'

Although it was Sunday I spent the morning scrubbing out the kitchen and threw open all the doors and windows in the place. Turned out the cupboards and lined them with clean paper. Washed the loose covers in the tin bath outside and spread them out on the bushes to dry.

'I'm going for a little aperitif,' Otley said.

Baldrics, I thought to myself, as I wiped the sweat from my forehead. It was about one o'clock when Steve called for the rats. Gordon was waiting for his Sunday dinner, and I watched Steve hurrying away with it, smartly dressed as he was going to church afterwards. Fawn, lightweight summer suiting, brown-and-white striped shirt, tasteful tie and tan leather shoes. A picture of decorum as he handed round the hymn books. I wondered if Miss Wintersgill had any idea of what he'd been up to as he dipped his hand into her bag of mint humbugs. Yet there was something strange about him. I didn't know what it was.

I made a nut roast and a bilberry pie while my husband was mafficking in the Rose & Crown. Then I prepared hedgerow greens for stir-frying, and smacked out ten *chapatis*, squatting outside in front of a large lump of millstone grit. There were more bilberries than I thought and when I got the pastry on top it was like Mount Everest. I had to take a shelf out of the oven to get it in.

I flopped into the squashy armchair and closed my eyes. The talking heads were going at it hammer and tongs with their thumbs up. Big bang. I heard as if in a dream. Free-falling dollar – Contras, blowpipes – Iranians have got Chinese silkworms – gross national product – Secretary General of the United Nations has got some teeth missing. Oh! no, that can't be right; he's going on a peace mission.

Otley shook me as a Eurocrat with an identikit face told us that every cow in the Common Market gets a grant of £250 a year. They can stand under the electricity pylons all day if they like. The Ministry of Agriculture and Fisheries issue guidelines but cows can't read. If I fill in a form and sign it Buttercup, will I get my £250?

Everything back to normal in Chernobyl. They just swish round with a hosepipe now and again. Not true that Sellafield's polluting the sea; they're just feeding the fish through that pipe under the water-line.

'Lying hounds,' said Otley, pulling his chair up to the table. 'That Geiger counter goes mad when I take it out there.'

'What can we do about it?' I asked. 'We're trapped.'

'Defeatist talk,' he said.

'There's no escape,' I went on. 'If we don't eat the food, we starve.'

'I'm not eating it,' he said.

I put the nut roast on the table and it looked like cattle-cake.

'There's some good gravy,' I said.

The greens had frizzled to nothing, waiting for the pubs to turn out.

I arranged them like the Japanese do, in a fancy pattern at the edge of the plates: three dandelion leaves and a glob of goutweed.

'If we eat it with chopsticks it'll last longer,' I suggested.

I made a mental note to pop down to the supermarket on the morrow.

I carried the bilberry mountain in triumph and put it on the table in the place of honour – before the master. It was brown pastry and hard as a petrified oak. I plunged the bread-knife into it and found it was hollow: a pie full of air, with a thin layer of bilberries on the bottom.

'Can't you do anything right?' said a disappointed Otley.

'I can't understand it,' I said. 'I filled it up to the top.'

'You can't have,' he complained.

'I did, I did,' I said. But cooking does funny things to food.

I remembered a cookery lesson at school when I made my first apple-dumpling, and ran all the way home with it for father's dinner. All there was left was dumpling round a big hole and a trail of stewed apple going back down the road.

I opened the oven door nervously and peered inside. There it was. A puddle of bilberry juice burnt into toffee on the oven floor.

'The bilberries are there,' I explained, looking at the pie again. 'It's just the juice that's gone.'

He seemed to be satisfied with this scientific analysis. It's one advantage of your husband not being able to cook. You can burn the corned-beef hash, put a few raisins in it and a spot of *garam masala* and call it Sri Lankan curry.

'Did he call for Mickey and Minnie?' he asked eventually, his eyes clouding over. I tried not to look him in the face, but I was afraid I might put the bilberry pie in his ear so I had to do.

'Yes,' I said. 'He was all dressed up and going to church; seemed like a nice young man.'

This bit of news cheered him up and I felt like Judas. But it was either me or them. If you're too nice you just cancel yourself out.

'Where's Serpentis?' I asked. 'He said they came from Serpentis.'

'It's a star. I've seen it through my telescope,' he said excitedly.

'I thought there was something silver about him,' I said.

'Told you, didn't I? They've been down here for yonks,' he said. 'And where d'you say he lives now?'

'Halifax,' I lied. 'Just up the road from the gibbet.'

'What's he doing here, then?' he asked.

'I don't know,' I said. 'It's not South Africa, you don't need a pass to come here.'

It being Sunday afternoon, Otley had a nap with the newspaper over his head. What a gay day! What shall I do? Play Patience? Darn socks? Clean the oven? Sew the master's buttons on? Bake a Victoria sponge?

26 July 2 AC

My dearest love has been called by one of his flock to rescue a frightened cat at the top of yonder poplar. The poor creature's pitiful cries have been heard for nigh on three days and nights. Help is at hand.

Birds singing! Bees buzzing! The world alive with joy. I

gather armsful of meadowsweet to strew o'er the kitchen floor. 'Twas a favourite of the Virgin Queen herself. I must tarry awhile in the cool shade of this friendly hedgerow, rampant with honeysuckle and pink bindweed. I fain would pick a nosegay but an enchantress lurks within. Deadly Nightshade with her purple frills.

> If I kiss you,
> Belladonna,
> I'll surely be
> A gonna.

Night falls and still my beloved has not returned. I hear the clang of the fire brigade on its way to get him. The cat has jumped down and Crispin is stuck in the tree. Gallant Crispin.

Your faithful servant awaits with the Hopel Popel done to a turn. I fear the kindling may be too heavy a burden my beloved. Leave half of it and go back for it tomorrow.

A painting of Crispin's hand reaching out towards the cat. A red fire-engine going through the traffic lights. More feathers and lady birds and then it was time for tea.

Otley was snoring away like billy-o with his mouth open. It was that period of gloom on a Sunday when everybody's sulking after the dinner-time quarrels, and there's nothing on the box but hymns of praise.

I thought we died every Sunday when I was little, and came alive again like Jesus. I used to sit very quietly on the prickly horsehair sofa, looking round at all the grannies and great-aunts and uncles in their best Sunday black, sleeping among the antimacassars and red-plush tablecloths. It was like the funeral parlour I passed on the way to school every day. Then, when the church bells started ringing, they woke up and had tinned peaches and cream and went for a walk.

I left Otley a note saying I'd gone over to High Riding and then went to see what Jeff was doing. What are Sundays on the Moon like? Are the do-it-yourself shops open? Can you use your free bus pass all day long? Would Jeff like a sample of a python? I'm entitled to know before I go for an awayday, and Otley will want to know what time the pubs open.

Thelma was drying some butterflies in the oven and then sticking them in rows in glass cases.

'I've got some of these,' she said, 'but there are regional variations.'

The tip of her tongue showed between tight lips as she sorted out the handwritten labels. 'Gatekeeper', she wrote, next to a brown-and-orange butterfly with a large, dark spot on each wing like a pair of sunglasses. 'Purple Hairstreak', she added underneath a scrap of burgundy gauze with a splodge of violet on one of its wings. She selected a long pin.

'Where's Sylvie?' I asked, feeling faint.

'Hanging round that Jeff, I expect. She's got it bad,' she said, smirking. 'Can't keep her hands off him – at her age an' all.'

'She's a late developer,' I said.

'It's like measles,' she went on. 'The older you are, the worse you get it.'

I daren't tell her I'd got it as well. I went into the garden to pick some flowers to replace my savaged ones. Cornflowers, phlox, marigolds and old-fashioned sweet peas made a cottage-garden bunch, to be crammed as they were picked into an earthenware jug. Someday, when I'm feeling precious I'll learn Japanese flower arranging and compose a Haiku, sitting before a single spray of cherry blossom:

> paradise blooming
> in a pink silken tassel
> vanishing too soon.

But there's not much call for that sort of thing round these parts, and you're not supposed to conduct the tea ceremony with Tetley's tea-bags. I searched in vain for Jeff and Sylvie.

What were those two up to? They weren't in the summer-house. Was she knitting that 'Doctor Who' scarf for him? Captain Kirk doesn't wear one. He wears a body-stocking. I wish Jeff would tell me when they were picking me up so I could put something decent on. My best twin-set and pearls and heather mixture classic tweed skirt from Marks & Spencer. I don't want them to think we're a load of riff-raff down here. And if they came on a Thursday I could have my hair done first as it's pensioners' day on Wednesday – thirty-five pence off. I hope they don't come today, that's all. I've still got my old jeans on that I scrubbed the kitchen floor in, and my 100 per cent cotton T-shirt, made in Madras, with a flap at the back to go over my dhoti.

It was a beautiful evening, the new moon lying on its back like a stranded beetle, surprised to see the sun not gone yet. I didn't want to go back home in case Otley asked me to make some sweet-and-sour soya chunks and Tandoori cabbage. So I went out through the bottom gate and down towards the canal. The towpath bright with blue meadow cranesbill, and white starry stitchwort, sewing a seam through the grass. A rusty old cruiser, the 'River Queen', lying abandoned, elder and rosebay willow-herb coming out through the roof.

Mr and Mrs Scattergood came towards me. Pink cheeks, grey hair and identical teeth and glasses. Married fifty years and never been apart. There was no need to talk, each knew what the other was thinking.

'How d'you do,' they said, in unison like galactic clones.

Then Mr and Mrs Pickersgill. He six foot plus and thin

as a lath, she five foot nothing and as broad as she was long. They had to talk to make contact as they couldn't see each other.

'Grand evening,' they said. Her from Venus and him from Mars.

Old Inky Pop with his dog, walking the same way and with the same shaped legs viewed from behind: flattened flanks, bowed out as far as the knees, two knobs, then coming in to meet at the ankles, another knob with feet attached at right angles. I've heard that people grow to look like their pets facially, but how does this apply to the back end?

'Ah doo,' he said. One to himself, he was. From an undiscovered planet.

I didn't expect to meet the Ancient Britons. Sunday was family day. Grandchildren to tea. Letters to write to daughters in New Zealand and Canada, and to sons in the Hong Kong police.

I was just going over the swing bridge by the old papermill when I saw this blue light flashing in the trees by the golf course. I went along the cart-track and down a snicket overgrown with ash and hawthorn, making a dark, green tunnel. The humming noise grew louder as I approached and then suddenly it stopped and the light went out. I emerged in a clearing and there it was! It looked like Recorder Five. I stood there, trying to locate a door I could knock on; then a beam of light hit me and I was inside the craft.

'Is that you, Jeff?' I inquired.

I looked round and recognized the star-map on the wall and the dispensers; there was the table they measured me on. Did they want the size of my shoes now? I took my flatties off just in case.

There was still no sign of anybody aboard and I was

standing at one of the port-holes looking over the tops of the trees towards Bradford when there was a whoosh! and we were airborne.

A jagged triangle appeared below us. That must be the British Isles. The curve of the Earth's surface could be seen as seas and continents dropped away. Then dark, like a black velvet curtain; and a shining blue-and-green globe, no more than a bauble on a Christmas tree.

'It's the most beautiful sight in the universe.'

I jumped at the sound of Jeff's voice and turned to find him at another window. A Kraak busy entering data into a computer squawked a welcome.

'I wish you'd told me,' I said. 'I've got my old jeans on, I look a right mess.'

'It was not planned for today. We were collecting specimens,' he said, 'but you turned up at the right time and in the right place.'

'These flowers'll die if you've got no water on the Moon,' I said, looking at them still clutched in my fist.

'We're trying to reproduce Earth conditions,' he said. 'They'll be all right once we get there.'

We seemed to arrive in the time it takes for a day trip to Skegness, putting down on one of the great plains. There was a sort of eerie light, the Earth rising full and casting blue-green shadows from the mountains.

'You have to be careful at full Earth,' Jeff warned. 'Some of them go mad.'

We left the Earthskimmer, clad in magnetic boots and all-in-one suits with head-pieces attached, bounding over the rocks like kangaroos.

'That's the Cordilleras,' Jeff said, pointing to a range of high mountains. 'Too late – you've missed them.'

'I wish I'd brought my camera,' I said.

'You can see the domes now,' he said, pointing to a glass city in the distance. 'A couple of jumps and we'll be home.'

A Kraak flew on ahead of us, flapping his wings lazily, his kangaroo legs tucked up neatly like the undercarriage of a plane.

'He has to fly,' Jeff explained. 'On foot, he'd bounce right over the top of those mountains.'

'Hasn't he got any boots?' I asked.

'He prefers to fly,' said Jeff, 'but he comes in handy for sending messages – two hops and he's there.'

The Moon-dust rose up in clouds under our feet, a fine, powdery, grey stuff like wood-ash. I thought it would be silver. Not a tree or a blade of grass to be seen. Vast dustbowls and sudden cliffs, rolling dunes and mountain ranges and then a flood of light as we came to the city.

We left our boots and suits in a lobby and I followed Jeff into a large hall where people were eating and drinking. They were very tall and fair, with high foreheads and cold grey-green eyes. It was hard to guess how old they were from their dress, or whether they were men or women. All wore a pale blue jogging suit and white plimsolls.

'This is Elin, my generation sister,' he said, pointing to one of the diners. She moved up and made a place for me. I was glad to sit down.

'What would you like?' she asked, putting a plate in front of me.

'I'm dying for a cup of tea,' I said.

'You Earthians are funny,' she said. 'It's the first thing you ask for when you get here.'

'Don't the Yanks want coffee, then?' I inquired.

'Oh! yes,' she said. 'There's a machine for espresso and cappuccino.'

I delved into my handbag and they all fell about laughing. I must have looked a mess as I hadn't had time to comb my hair or anything, my shirt lap was hanging out and I was carrying a bunch of drooping flowers. I put my hand in my pocket for a tissue. They might not wipe their noses here. Jeff said he would show me round the botanic gardens when I'd eaten.

'All right,' I said, 'but I have to go back tomorrow – it's washday.'

THE EARTH SHONE against a black velvet sky and a million stars, bright with a steady silver light, sprinkled the sky around her. It was funny to think of Otley down there eating his cheese 'n' onion crisps and watching *Sports Special* on BBC 2.

The gardens were a sort of miniature Kew with plants from all over the world in their own micro-climate. Hot, steamy jungle with dripping leaves and exotic orchids. Cold alpines in neat clumps on the rocks. Dry desert with prickly, geometric shapes. The temperate zone with meadow flowers and a shady bluebell wood.

'I had no idea,' I said. 'It's just like Middleton Woods at Ilkley.'

'We've been in your area for some time now,' he said. 'Before that I was in Siberia.'

'That must have been a bit nippy,' I said.

'It's beautiful in the summer – one of our favourite places,' he went on. 'We draw lots to go there.'

'Never!' I said.

'Acres of virgin forest, fields golden with buttercups, salmon in Lake Baikal; it's paradise,' he said.

'Well, I'll be jiggered!' I said. 'I thought it was all salt mines.'

'But it's getting polluted now, like everywhere,' he added.

'How d'you find your way there?' I inquired, trying to look as if I knew something about navigation.

'We follow the Trans-Siberian railway,' he said.

'I thought you followed ley lines,' I said. 'Something to do with magnetism.' I was only parroting what Heron had told me.

'The old ones did in their starships, but it's easier for us to go along the canals and railways,' he said, stopping to admire a sunflower.

'What about before they were built?' I asked.

'We had the Roman roads,' he said, 'and the green track-ways.'

'They'll soon have finished the Aire Valley trunk road,' I said, 'from Kendal to Doncaster; goes past Damart if you want to pop in for some thermal underwear.'

He told me a lot of things that you'd have to be a scientist to understand. But I knew what he meant by hot and cold. The Moon, he said, is like the Sahara desert, only worse: freezing at night and scorching hot during the day. The people only leave the city if they have to.

Selenus, the first colony, was built inside one of the great craters. It could be lowered further down in the daytime when the sun was at its hottest. At night the inhabitants came up again to see the lunar lights from the viewing gallery. A lift took us up to the top of a glass tower.

'It's like the Telecom Tower,' I said, as we watched the sun's corona light up the horizon bright as a 250-watt, pearl long-life bulb. This petered out, to be followed by a 'firework' display.

Red flames licked the sky as if it were bonfire night and just above our heads hung Earth, a huge, dazzling, blue-and-silver Chinese lantern. They'd never believe me when I got back home.

'There's not much to see here,' Jeff explained, 'but the sky makes up for it.'

The beautiful ones, the Selenites, were the first here, he told me; then the Kraaks arrived from the Swan constellation. They built an extension for them, like Lord Snowdon's aviary at the London Zoo, and they settled down happily. The snake people from Serpentis took longer to fit in. They brought their serpent god with them and frightened everybody out of their wits.

'What happened?' I asked, wondering if Steve was one of them.

'It was killed in a fight with a Kraak; they spend a lot of their time on Earth now,' Jeff went on. 'They like to be with the snakes.'

It looked as if he was.

I was beginning to feel tired and asked to be shown to my room. I hoped there would be hot and cold water and a teasmaid but didn't like to ask. Elin took me down a long corridor with cubicles at each side. A door slid open and I was in a bright little room with white walls, a pale green carpet on which there was a yellow sleeping bag, and a painted ceiling in blues and pinks, like an Earth sky. Elin's eyes were like river pearls.

'We want you to feel at home,' she said, with a twisted smile.

She took the flowers from me, saying they would go into a reviver, coming out as good as new. I was a bit scared of being alone and felt comforted by the feel of the gun in my handbag. She saw what I was doing and shook her head angrily.

'We don't allow guns here,' she said, making a move towards me.

'You had them in *Star Wars*, hadn't you?' I said, holding on to it.

'I'll put it in here, then,' Elin said, pointing to a wall safe, 'as you're just staying one night; and if you'd like a dry-clean . . .'

'Can I have two aspirins and some water? I've got a headache,' I said, holding my head in my hands to demonstrate my meaning. She put her hand on my forehead, it was as cool and refreshing as the mountain dew and when she took it away my headache had gone. Another smile and she was gone too. What was it about that smile that made me feel uneasy?

I undressed and went behind a curtain with the dry-cleaner. There were two buttons, one red and one blue, which meant off and on in any language. I pressed the red one and a jet of fine powder like Fuller's Earth smothered me from head to foot. It felt as if I had been touched by angels' wings. Then I pressed the blue button and the powder was all sucked inside the dry-cleaner again. I brushed my hair vigorously with a round, hard brush that I found on a ledge, and hoped it wasn't a scrubbing brush. My skin felt 'silky' and my hair shone like burnished gold. It was much better than the watering-can shower.

I lay for a while looking at the ceiling, wondering what they were doing down below. Had they missed me yet? Had Otley taken the washing in off the bushes? Had he turned off the pauper's pottage? I didn't want to find the house burnt down when I got back. The insurance only covers acts of God. Otley would be pleased at my initiative, though, and I might even get on *Parkinson One-to-One*.

'We'll go for a jump after breakfast,' Jeff said, the next morning.

'Oh! that'll be nice,' I said, finishing my muesli and bananas.

We put our boots and suits on in the lobby and went

outside. It was still dark. I don't know how they tell night from day. Jeff said the sky was always black. We went bounding over the mountains, hand in hand.

'That's the Rook Mountains,' Jeff said, pointing downwards. 'We've just gone over the Cordilleras.'

'Why didn't you say?' I asked him. 'I'd have had a better look.'

'That's Billy,' he said, pointing to a crater.

I bounced on to the rim to have a good view of the inside and felt myself falling into it in slow motion as if I were in an action replay on *Match of the Day*. I came to rest near the bottom on a bed of bluish dust that spread out in ripples, like the sand when the tide's gone out.

'That was a stupid thing to do,' said Jeff, as he came down in three hops to help me up.

'I felt as if I was flying,' I said. 'It was lovely.'

'If you fall into one of those cracks we'll never get you out,' he said, pointing to a deep, narrow ravine. Well, ravine's not the right word – more of a chink, it was, one of many radiating out between the craters, like a gigantic dart-board.

'Let's go back, then,' I said, shivering. 'How deep are they?'

'A mile or more,' he said. 'We think there's water down there, and monsters; the children went out one day with their teacher, exploring; they never came back.'

'How awful,' I said, moving into the protection of his magnetic field.

'It is forbidden to leave the city now,' he went on, 'but we show visitors round; there are so many Earthmen anyway, one or two wouldn't be missed.'

'Well, thank you very much,' I said. 'I've taken the trouble to come all this way to see where you live, and that's the thanks I get.'

'Oh! I didn't mean you. I was speaking generally,' he said hastily.

Although I couldn't see him properly in his insulating outfit, I could absorb the magnetism that seemed to surround him. I could have leapt over the moonscape for ever with him. The sun was getting hotter and Jeff said it was time we bounced back home.

'That's Pico,' he said, pointing to a beautiful white peak in the distance. 'Our Moon goddess.'

'Ooh! lovely,' I said, blinking at the dazzling light.

When we got back to the city he took me to see the laboratories where they keep the Earth specimens. His silver-blue eyes lit up as he looked at the beautiful birds and butterflies and the many herbs and flowers growing in profusion: yellow canaries, green parakeets, gaudy red-and-blue macaws, blackbirds and woodpeckers.

'As you can see, these are living laboratories,' he explained. 'The moon is dead, a fossil which we have to bring to life.'

'Why don't you stay with us?' I said. 'Save yourselves the bother.'

'We only want the best,' he said. 'We don't want all the garbage that's down there – we pick what we want.'

'We've got litter-bins now, and bottle-banks,' I said. 'People are becoming more socially aware.'

'It's filthy,' he said. 'You've got that nice planet and you're making it into a rubbish dump.'

'It's not my fault,' I said. 'I put all my rubbish in the bin.'

'Don't take it personally,' he said. 'I'm speaking intergalactically.'

'Well, all right, then,' I said, moving closer. I still didn't know what he was made of. When I accidentally bumped into him once he made a clank like an aluminium saucepan.

'How old are you?' he asked suddenly.

'I'm in my second childhood,' I said.

'You're only a baby,' he said. 'I'm in my tenth child-hood.'

'Thelma has some butterflies and a dragonfly missing,' I said. 'Have you got them?' She would be mad if she knew they were up here.

'They're in the reviving chamber,' he said. 'Don't tell her.'

He showed me the nursery next where infant Selenites were learning to play the violin, their solemn little faces engrossed in the bowing and scraping. They got the idea from Japan. They were taught ancestor worship as well encouraged by paintings of the Great Voyage of Discovery from Eridani that decorated the walls. There were no nuclear families. Children were hard to come by on the moon, so you got them when you could – sometimes from a test-tube and sometimes from a bawdy night out in the botanic gardens. Jeff said he didn't mind which.

My hopes of a silver baby were dashed when I found out that the Selenites produced them in the usual doggy fashion. You'd think they'd have something better than that. How does Jeff go on, then, if he's made of aluminium? Perhaps he keeps them in a sardine tin.

The colony was much larger than I had thought, the city being only the central core. There were also grain fields and farms and the starport where selected candidates were pre-paring for deep-freeze emigration to Mars. Did I want to see it? he asked. I said I had to be getting back to Earth, as the dirty dishes would be piling up in the sink. I thought of the slave-ships taking the Africans to work on the planta-tions. Is that why they've got me up here? To put me in the deep-freeze and ship me off to Mars to work on the canals. You can't trust anybody.

'What time is the next saucer back?' I asked.

'I was hoping you'd stay a bit longer,' he said. 'You'll like it here once you get used to it.'

The magnetism was wrapping me round again. I had only to look into his eyes and I was lost. There was that video again: the beautiful people up in the stars, making butterflies and playing the violin as they spin through the galaxy, scattering moonbeams. Nights in the botanic gardens. Morning jumps in the mountains. Watching the Earth rise. Earth, my home! I must get back. Otley will be waiting for his clean shirts – 'Haven't you sewn my buttons on yet?' he'll ask me as soon as I get in – and he'll be wearing a red sock and a blue one.

'I'll come again another day,' I said. 'Thanks for inviting me; I have enjoyed it.' I might have been at the vicarage garden party.

'You can book a place now if you want, while you're here,' he said.

'What place?' I inquired, thinking of a nice bungalow at Scarborough.

'For when the Earth's at a standstill, clogged up with rubbish,' he said. 'When the water's polluted and the land poisoned, you'll all be wanting to come and there's only room for a few.'

'Oh! I never thought about that,' I said.

'You'll be lucky to get in,' he said.

'What would I be doing, then?' I asked him, wondering what sort of jobs they had for Ancient Britons in their second childhood.

'You can go round with the tea-trolley,' he said.

'Oh!' I said, trying to hide my disappointment.

'What did you want to do then?' he asked.

'Well, if I could go in the reviver for an hour or two,' I said, 'I could start all over again; I could . . .' I didn't know how to say it.

'You could what?' he asked.

'I . . . well, I've always wanted a Moonchild,' I said. He nodded eagerly.

He must be leading a double life, I thought; up and down, up and down, like a yo-yo. A girl on every planet. Who was that Elin?

'Are you married?' I asked, holding my breath.

'No,' he said.

'I'm glad you're not,' I said. 'I don't want to come between you.'

'There are no tribal rituals here,' he said. 'We have generation sisters, six to each generator.'

'Who's Elin?' I asked. 'Where does she come in?'

'She's a first-generation sister,' he said. 'She's responsible for training the novices in how to maintain the generator.'

I looked round and couldn't see any sign of a diesel anywhere.

'Where is it?' I said.

'Where's what?' he said, a bit baffled-looking.

'The diesel,' I said.

'There's no diesels up here,' he said. Now I was mystified.

'You just said there was a generator, didn't you?' I reminded him.

'Oh! that's me,' he said. 'I'm a people-generator.'

If he means what I think he means, I mused, I'm going to have to ask the sixty-four-thousand-dollar question.

'What do you . . .? Where do you . . .? I mean, how do you . . .?' I stammered.

'Oh! in the usual way,' he said. 'Like they do on Channel 4.'

I suppose I must have looked embarrassed, because I wasn't expecting all that dirty-raincoat stuff on the Moon. She always looks so pure and virginal.

'Oh! well, I'd better be going,' I said, picking up my handbag.

'It's like stock-breeding,' he said. 'Just a few of us came from Eridani and we have to maintain the herd.'

'I was hoping to buy a silver baby in a silver egg,' I said, 'but I'll make a donation to the Sports Fund instead.'

That was only a part of his work, though. He supervised the sample-collecting and was the Minister for Propaganda. He had to make sure we Earthians knew the score, even if it meant kidnapping us and bringing us up here. For one thing they didn't want us rushing to the Moon all at once, when we've messed up our own planet. There's a housing shortage there as well.

I said goodbye to the dear little Selenites, who were so pretty, like dolls with their porcelain faces and spun-gold hair. They asked permission to come and see me off, and came bobbing after me as if on pogo sticks. The saucer was waiting with one of the Kraaks on board, who was going to see what he could pick up on Ilkley Moor and could drop me in Boggle's Field by the beck. Jeff had to attend a board meeting and said he would see me on bank holiday Monday, if not before.

It was hard to break out of his magnetic field and in the end he had to push me into the flying saucer. I could understand how it was that he had got to be the Chief Generator.

'Cheerio!' I called. 'Don't do anything I wouldn't do.'

But I knew he would. I might as well have saved my breath.

We shot away towards the beautiful Chinese lantern hanging in the black velvet sky. I watched through the port-hole until that bluish-green dust and stark mountain ranges turned into our silver Moon again. The Kraak came towards me with his dipstick, blinking his basalt eyes.

'You're not going to poke that thing in my ear again, are you?' I said.

His feathers ruffled up round his neck making him look like Good Queen Bess. I wondered if I dare ask him for one. He looked in my left ear and raised the dipstick.

'You've done that once,' I said. 'It's my feet you didn't get.' I pointed to my feet and nodded, pointed to my ears and shook my head. He did it the other way round. Perhaps he'd lost his bit of paper with it written down. I was always losing my shopping list. He measured my ears once again and seemed fascinated by my earrings. Perhaps he had some magpie in him. I took one out and gave it to him and he hopped round the cabin with it in his beak, then hooked it on to the dipstick where it stayed. I felt sorry for him and stroked his ruffled feathers.

'Can I have one?' I asked him. He opened his beak to answer me.

'Kraak,' he said.

I watched through the port-hole as the twinkling lights of Bradford sprang up at us. It was dark here as well as on the Moon. We nearly hit Lister's mill chimney as we came in low skimming over the tree-tops. No sooner had I picked out the line of traffic on the Keighley road than I was in Boggle's Field and the flying saucer was just another star in the sky.

I was still holding my bunch of flowers as if I were a magician and had pulled them out of a hat. I had no idea of the time and looked through a cottage window to see what was on television. A woman came out and chased me away with a sweeping-brush, but not before I had caught a glimpse of crazy turrets in an eerie light. A haunted house like the one in *Psycho* and a doom-laden voice rang out on the airwaves. It must be *Their Lordships' House*. It was the witching hour!

THE COTTAGE WAS in
darkness when I got there. At least Otley wasn't sitting up
biting his nails. He must have taken his Mogadons and
retired. I tried the door but it seemed to be locked. I
thought I heard a scuffling noise and then the lights went
on. It was a pity to wake him up but he would be pleased
when he knew where I'd been to. He was a firm believer in
private enterprise. Suddenly the bedroom window opened
on its rickety hinges and two heads looked out. One went
back in again quickly.

'Let me in,' I called. 'I've been in a flying saucer and I'm
worn out with jet lag.'

Presently the door opened and a holdall came hurtling
out hitting the tin bath with a deafening clang and bringing
on my migraine. He was no respecter of persons. I picked
up the bag and peered at the label tied to it. It could have
been written by a bad-tempered spider.

'May Craven', it said, in weedy black capitals. 'Of no
fixed abode'.

I hammered on the door in a panic. I was dying for a cup of tea. 'Let me in; let me in,' I wailed, like the ghost of Cathy in *Wuthering Heights*. 'I've been to the moon and I've got a splitting headache.'

'Serves you bloody well right,' my husband called back.

There was a squeaking, twittering sound and then more scuffling.

'Can I have a drink of water and some aspirins, then?' I pleaded.

'Strumpet, bawdy-basket, I've finished with you for good this time,' he said. 'Go back to the moon for your aspirins.'

Suddenly the door opened and I staggered into the kitchen. Otley was standing there with a face like thunder.

'You've been gone three days,' he said. 'And all I've had to eat is that pauper's pottage stuff, it's like senna pods in fish-glue.'

'You said I could go if I got the chance, didn't you?' I reminded him.

'Yes, but I didn't think you would,' he said.

I poured out some tea and flopped into the squashy chair. He was wearing a silk dressing-gown that I had not seen before and he had love bites on his neck. More scuffling noises came from upstairs.

'Is there someone else?' I queried.

'Yes there is!' he snapped. 'D'you expect me to live like a Pope? I'm sick of going round to the Marriage Guidance Council.'

'I'm tired,' I said. 'I want to go to bed. These flying saucers make you dizzy.'

'You're not sleeping here,' he said. 'Go back to where you've been these last two nights.'

'I can't,' I said. 'There isn't another saucer until tomorrow.'

'Pull the other leg – it's got bells on,' he said.

I was too tired to fight when he pushed me through the

door, so I picked the holdall up and trudged wearily down through the cabbages.

'And don't come back here upsetting Bella,' he called after me. 'She's very highly-strung.'

I knocked on the door at High Riding and it creaked open to reveal Sylvie, a drooping butterfly with folded wings. Sad blue eyes, hooded, like harebells looking down; wisps of hair like the silken feathers of a Christmas-tree bird; wearing a satin kimono embroidered with the symbols of long life and happiness. A picture of red-and-blue despair.

'I've been thrown out,' I told her. 'Can I sleep here for a while?'

I followed her upstairs and along the murky passage where she took care not to let her eyes rest on the Big Daddies hanging on the wall.

'Have you seen Jeff lately?' she asked, when she had found me a bed.

'He's on the Moon,' I said. 'He commutes between us and them.'

'I knew there was something funny about him,' she said. 'He kissed me once and it sizzled, like when you spit on an iron to see if it's hot enough.'

'He's hard as well, isn't he?' I said. 'Hard as a corset-stiffener.'

'I know,' she drooled. 'When you get anywhere near him it's like being stunned by a magnetic piledriver.'

Silly old fool, I thought. At her age.

'He's got a woman up there, you know,' I said. 'Well, six, in fact.'

She turned on me like a fury, face contorted, arms flailing, hair swishing like the tail of a rocking-horse ridden by a mad three-year-old.

'Liar!' she screamed. 'You want him yourself; I'll kill you if you take him away from me.' This romantic streak runs through the family.

'We're just good friends,' I said, 'like Bill and Ben the Flowerpot Men.' I took the pot of African violets that she was going to brain me with.

'I've waited all my life for a man who doesn't smell like a Big Daddy,' she said. 'I can't stand all that beer and tobacco coming out of their sweat-glands; styptic pencils and Brut on a Sunday; jingling their keys in their pockets while they wait for the newspaper man.'

'I expect he's made of teflon-coated aluminium,' I said. 'That's why.'

'I don't care if he's made of polystyrene,' she said. 'Just as long as he doesn't smell like a scented compost heap.'

'There's no need to fight over him,' I told her. 'They don't get married up there; they have generation sisters, as many as they want.'

'Like the King of Siam?' she asked. She piled her hair on top of her head and did a polka round the room. 'We're doing that. I'm playing Anna and all Sammy Chandra's relations are in it.'

'They'll just be right,' I said.

'As long as they don't have to show their legs,' she added.

'If we both go up there and they put us in the reviver, we can be generation sisters as well,' I said. At once she changed from a polka-dot governess into a feral feline as she picked up the letter opener with 'A Present from More-cambe' engraved on it.

'I'll kill you first,' she said. 'I want him all to myself.'

'Well, I think I'll turn in, I've got a headache,' I said, reading the inscription on the knife, 'I could do with a few days in Morecambe, I'll get some money out of the Post Office tomorrow.'

'I'll come with you,' she said, changing yet again. 'It's a long time since I've been there; not since the chapel outing when Brinley Theopholus went down in the quicksands.'

Well, I had nowhere else to go. Nobody wanted me.

Everybody was having a meaningful relationship. I might as well have a meaningful relationship with myself. Sylvie can suit herself in what she does.

'You're not bringing your knitting, are you?' I inquired. In the past she had ruined many a picnic clicking away like Madame Defarge; warning us all to keep away from her wool; sticking her needles in the pork pies.

'Supposing it rains,' she said. 'I shall have nothing to do.'

We decided to wait for the Sunday coming, which was a Blue Day. It's the new system on British Rail. If you go on a Blue Day it's cheaper than going on a White Day; and if you see a carriage window with a sticker on you can get in there for only £2 extra, first class and with white linen squares to lean on.

'With a bit of luck we might get a sticker,' I said.

I would have to go down home for a few goods and chattels as I didn't want to go with my shirt-lap hanging out.

'See you in the morning, then,' Sylvie said, putting out the lamp.

I looked out of the window high up on the roof: chimneys loomed like zombies fresh from their voodoo graves, trees crept up from the valley like a black fungus with lights strung in their branches bright as diamonds in a Nubian's hair, and the rolling fells nuzzled the high moor like a litter of pups. Suddenly, a golden dazzle zig-zagged across the sky, but I didn't know if it was a flying saucer or the migraine.

The next morning I went up to the cottage for my diary and my painting things. Bella was doing some bacon and eggs and Otley had a very satisfied look about him, like a camel who has just bitten his dragoman.

'I thought I told you not to come back here,' he said.

Bella tossed her long black mane like a tetchy filly in her first race. I must be careful not to alarm her.

'It's just my diary I want,' I said soothingly, 'and my paints – you didn't pack them.'

'Bella's read it,' he said. 'She says she's seen you with Crispin; you'll be hearing from my solicitor.'

'Oh!' I said. This was a surprise as I didn't know he had one.

'Is that all you've got to say for yourself?' he asked, as if I'd been caught with my fingers in the till.

'I've told you, there's no Crispin, it's all in the mind – you know, like Martin Chuzzlewit,' I said, eyeing the breakfast hungrily.

'Who's he?' Bella asked. 'Anyway, I've met Crispin down the pub.'

'He's coming up here so you can meet him face to face,' Otley said. 'What have you got to say to that?'

I took my diary and left. I just wanted to get back to my painting. They can have their love bites and their bacon and eggs. I hope they get gallstones. Perhaps I could get some food at the big house.

Thelma and Sylvie glared at each other over the Rose's lime marmalade. Sylvie wanted Golden Shred; Mummy always had it on Sundays, didn't she? Thelma would only eat lime marmalade because, she said, it saved her life when she was in Rangoon. Suffering from Delhi-belly, it was all she could eat on dry toast, and she had been faithful to it ever since.

'Why don't you get both?' I asked them, wolfing it on some toast.

'We do when I do the shopping,' Sylvie said, 'but she went this time.'

'I'm going down the village. I'll bring you some back,' I said.

The lads were picking caterpillars off the cabbages, leaderless. What would Jeff be doing now? Generating? How many of those little Selenites could he keep in his sardine

tin? And who had the key? I would have to think about
booking a seat up there. It's getting full up down here, all
right. If you go anywhere on a bank holiday there's a
queue ten miles long for a cup of tea.

'Don't you think you should see a doctor?' Mike said,
when I called to see him. He was dressed as a Samurai and
Heron had his Maid of the Mountains stuff on with his long
beads.

'Why?' I asked. 'I'm all right.'

'Dad was down here. He says you keep on about a bloke
called Crispin and you said you went to the Moon last
Sunday; he was just about at the end of his rope.'

'I did. I did,' I told him. 'I jumped over the Cordilleras,
fell down a crater called Billy, and watched the Earth rise
with the Chief Generator – it's the same bloke who does the
morris dancing up at High Riding.'

'You know, you're driving him into somebody else's
arms,' Mike said.

'He drives himself,' I said. 'Always has done.'

'It's six of one and half a dozen of the other,' he said, like
an old granny. 'You both want a good leathering.'

'Well, I can speak for my half dozen and he can speak for
his,' I said.

'Dad said if you came down here I've got to keep you
here.' Mike nodded at Heron and Heron nodded back.
What did that mean? Was it a signal to get a ticket to San
Francisco? I went upstairs and looked in the attic. Dirty
socks, old *Private Eyes* and *Beanos*. Everything seemed to be
normal: wet towels on the floor in the bathroom, records
and Y-fronts under the beds, dirty mugs on the bedside
tables, guitars, keyboards, synthesizer, speakers, plugs, adap-
tors and enough wiring to garrotte a Spanish army. Nothing
out of the ordinary that I could see. Perhaps they'd hidden
their Nazi uniforms under the floorboards. I got down on

my hands and knees and tapped round the skirting boards and lifted up the edges of the carpets. Nothing there. I crawled out into the passage and went all the way along feeling for loose planks.

The midday sun came in through the stained-glass window of Queen Victoria driving a steam-engine. Red, blue, green and gold lights shot from her robes making little rainbows on the walls. Her Imperial Majesty looked down in disdain as I scrabbled about on my knees. It was all right for her – she'd get an equerry to do this sort of thing. Suddenly there were footsteps on the stairs, and before I realized what was happening two men in white coats grabbed hold of me and I was bundled out into an ambulance. Mike and Otley got in as well and we all sat looking at each other: Mike in his Samurai outfit; Otley with his telescope and his Geiger counter, disappearing hair standing on end; me with my tattered old jeans, shirt-lap that would keep hanging out, and handbag with a toy gun in it. How would they know which one of us was mad?

'I've got to get some Golden Shred for Sylvie,' I announced.

Nobody answered. We screeched past the traffic lights at red.

'She's saving the golliwogs for a badge,' I said.

Still no answer. We skidded round a corner and came to a halt.

'Do you speak English?' I asked.

They found a doctor who did. He was Asian. He shuffled a bundle of papers and kept extracting one like somebody doing a card-trick.

'How long have you been having these hallucinations?' he asked.

'What hallucinations?' I asked him back. His eyes met Otley's.

'How did you get on with your mother?' he tried next.

'I loved her,' I said; he smiled at me and put that paper away.

'Except when she sang and then I hated her,' I told him.

He got the paper out again, ran his finger down the page and looked up. 'It says here that when you were five you said you wished she were dead, then you could go out to play.' His finger left the page and pointed in my direction. His round face loomed at me like a harvest moon.

'Yes,' I said. 'Jimmy Stott was outside cracking tar-bubbles.'

He leaned forward blowing a blast of *garam masala* in my face. 'And your father?'

'What about him?' I asked.

'You buried him in the sand at Bridlington and the fire-brigade had to get him out before the tide came in and drowned him.'

'Yes,' I said.

'That wasn't a very nice thing to do, was it?' he scolded.

'No,' I said. 'Him in his best suit an' all.'

'Then what made you do it?' he asked anxiously.

'He switched the wireless off when I was listening to Uncle Mac on *Children's Hour*,' I said, remembering it very clearly.

'It seems you have exhibited schizophrenic tendencies from an early age,' he said, looking at Otley for confirmation.

'She has,' he said.

'You keep a diary in which you mention your lover Crispin, yet you deny his existence,' he went on, like Perry Mason.

'He's made up. There's no such person,' I assured him.

The door opened and Bella came in with Steve Hurst. She was wearing a neat grey frock with a white collar, her hair tied back in a bun. Steve was in a navy-blue blazer and grey flannels, like a school prefect.

'What's your name?' Otley asked him.

'Crispin,' he said.

I should have said who he was and where I met him, but I didn't want Otley to know what I'd done with the rats. Bella looked very pleased and snuggled up to Otley and they gazed into each other's eyes. Steve looked the other way and avoided me.

'Have you ever been caught shoplifting?' he asked me next.

'Yes,' I said. 'The government encourages private enterprise.'

'When?' the good doctor wanted to know.

'When I was hungry and had no money,' I said.

'That's no excuse,' he said. 'We must maintain law and order.'

'What do you expect me to do, then, starve to death?' I asked.

'It's her age,' Otley said. 'Can't you give her some hormones or something?'

'I don't want any hormones,' I protested. 'I like my age. I don't want to go back, not down here anyway.'

'And she says she's been to the Moon,' Otley said, like a telltale-tit.

'I have,' I said. 'They gave me a lovely dry-clean. You ask Jeff.'

'My wife's gone doolally-tap,' Otley went on.

'As did your army in the days of the Raj. It is indeed sad,' replied the doctor. 'Perhaps a little holiday might help.'

'I'm going to Morecambe on Sunday,' I said, 'with Sylvie.'

'There's no need to have her in here, not yet anyway, but keep your eye on her,' he told Otley. He doesn't know he'll be busy keeping his eye on Bella. Mike put his arm round my shoulders and steered me through the door. It must be serious for him to do that.

'I don't know what all this is about,' I told them. 'You've all seen the UFOs over High Riding.'

'Yes, but we don't keep saying we've been up in one,' Mike said.

'I'm booking a place for us next time I go, before it gets full up,' I said. 'Do you want to be a generator, Mike, or would you rather register with a sperm bank?'

'How d'you mean?' he asked, feigning innocence with his gypsy eyes.

'Well, I don't want you going off to San Francisco with the bifocals. I want some posterity to leave my diary to,' I blurted out. I was afraid I might have offended him but he just laughed.

'Oh! wait till I tell Heron that,' he said.

'Well?' I waited for an answer but none came.

'Well, what?' Mike asked, his face twisted as if in agony.

'Are you, or are you not, going to San Francisco?' I demanded.

He laughed till he cried then wiped his eyes on Mummy's shirt-lap.

'We might go for a holiday,' he said, as soon as he was able.

30 July 2 AC

Gallant Crispin away at dawn with nary a glance at his gruel. He is to lend a hand bell-ringing with the Middle Thump Clangers and must needs practise his pull. 'Tis a dampish day and the elfin kind are at work threading diamonds on the spider-webs. The dandelions hang their heads waiting for the sun and the butterflies are grounded. A drowsy Skipper hides in the undergrowth, his wings folded, pretending to be a moth:

> Come out, I've seen you,
> Dingy Skipper,
> Lurking about,
> Like the Yorkshire Ripper.

My beloved comes limping home with one leg longer than the other. It seems he was lending an ear to a troubled clanger and missed his pull; the rope caught his ankle and hoisted him up to the belfry where he dangled until they changed the tune. Forsooth! he is accident-prone. Mercifully, his semolina pudding and rose-hip syrup is bubbling in the bain-marie. Methinks he hath forgotten the kindling. Lack-a-day! my lopsided love.

More feathers and ladybirds and Crispin hanging in the belfry like a large stick-insect. After all the trouble I'm taking I shall be very annoyed if Mike doesn't get me some posterity. I don't want my life's work mouldering away in a shoe-box under the library, until somebody from Brent discovers it and burns it for being sexist and racist. It's funny Pauline doing a bunk; she must know something. It's no good asking Mike – he only laughs. He listens to his father because he's a war hero, but Otley's attending to Bella these days; he's got no time for poofters. Sylvie's not speaking to Thelma because she had *Wozzeck* on when she wanted to watch *Blankety Blank*; if I don't get her away they'll murder each other. She's pining for Jeff poor soul; I daren't tell her he loves me. Living with the Hawkweed clan is like trying to knit a jumper with somebody unravelling the other end and with the cat chasing after the wool. It all gets a bit much. Still, I'm enjoying being a wok-widow for a few days until Otley gets fed up of Bella's Bombay duck.

There was a damp mist hanging about on Sunday morning when Sylvie and I hopped on a Hoppa down to the station. It was a bit off-putting, but when we heard on the news that they were dying of the heat in Greece it cheered us up a bit – no fear of that in Morecambe.

'Two Blue Days to Morecambe, please,' I said, through a round hole.

'Blue Days haven't started yet,' said the booking clerk, consulting his manual. 'Don't start till October.'

'But we've got a leaflet,' Sylvie protested, waving it at him.

'You haven't read it, have you?' he said accusingly.

'Can we have a Sticker, then?' I asked him.

'You can't book Stickers – you have to run after 'em,' he said, with a sigh, as if he were addressing an inebriated chipmunk.

'Haven't you got anything off, then?' I asked anxiously.

'You can have an Early Bird to Carlisle if you get up in time to catch the 06.34,' he said, studying his literature.

'That's a bit too early for us,' I said.

'What about a Round Robin, then?' he suggested, riffling the pages like a Mississippi gambler dealing cards. 'Lancaster, Carlisle, Skipton – any way round.'

'That sounds all right,' Sylvie said, turning to me.

'Sorry, that's only Monday to Thursday,' he said.

We waited expectantly as a long queue formed behind us.

'Hurry up, then! Make your mind up,' somebody shouted.

'Go back to bed if you don't know what to do,' came a voice from behind us.

They were most unfair, the booking clerk was only doing his job.

He took a deep breath 'Freedom of the North West Rover? Anywhere you like between Liverpool, Manchester, Leeds and Carlisle; £24 for seven days' riding.'

'That's too much riding about. She gets migraine going to Bradford on the bus,' Sylvie said, pointing at me. I nodded in agreement.

'You can have a Sprinter to Blackpool on the Roses Rail Link,' he said, warming to his subject. 'It says here it's your smartest move yet.'

'That sounds nice,' I said, 'but we really wanted to go to Morecambe.'

'Then go to bloody Morecambe!' An irate voice told us from behind.

We booked our tickets and Sylvie said she'd brought her Post Office book if I hadn't got enough money with me.

'Sleep under the bloody pier,' our adviser called after us.

'Aren't some people rude,' Sylvie observed, as we stumbled down the steps and on to the train. Soon, we were in the 'basket of eggs' country round Gargrave and Hellifield, the rolling drumlins with their wooded frills like a ballet dancer's tu-tu, rising up out of the mist. If the windows were cleaner we'd be able to see them better. In Switzerland they've got little goblins in white coats running up and down the platforms washing the windows every time you stop.

'Tickets please!' shouted an official dressed like a sergeant in the Japanese Imperial Guard. We were taken by surprise and rummaged frantically about our persons. I couldn't help noticing that everybody had a different ticket. Some had long pink ones; others had little brown ones; large, square red and yellow ones; oblong white ones with purple edging; Day Rovers; Metro-Permits; Student Railcards; Family Railcards; Senior Citizen Railcards; Weekend Savers; Big City Savers. Clunk-click, every trip.

A swarthy son of the desert pushed past wearing dark glasses and what looked like a checked tea-towel on his head. He gave us a funny look.

'What's he doing going to Morecambe?' Sylvie wanted to know.

'Otley says they're after our water,' I informed her.

'Might be collecting for his harem – we'd better watch out,' Sylvie said, getting out her knitting. I think she's worrying unnecessarily. I've read a lot of desert romances and all you have to say is 'You can't do this to me – I'm British.'

Sylvie's needles clicked away through the limestone scars of Giggleswick, which were gleaming like the whitened bones of dinosaurs; through the caving country round Ingleborough and then into alien territory: the Red Rose county itself. I began to feel uneasy, half-expecting to be bludgeoned with a cricket-bat at any minute. It's a psychological block akin to the Iron Curtain. I'm not staying long.

'I want to go on the Big Wheel,' Sylvie said, jumping up and down.

The Hawkweeds always get excited when they see a fairground. When Otley was six weeks old his father took him on the roundabouts, tucking him under his arm, like a pound of sausages. We've often thought that might be why he's disorientated. That and the ball-bearings in his head from the war.

We found a Bed & Breakfast place near the Central Pier so that we could join in the open-air dancing. Otley always insisted on going in a caravan as you don't have to keep saying please and thank you, and smile at everybody, so it was a nice change.

There was so much to do! Roller skating? But we daren't try that again because the last time we went we pulled all the safety-rails up falling down. Miss Great Britain contest? That would give us an inferiority complex. A bowls tournament? But like Khrushchev we think humanity's face is more interesting than its backside. Just thinking about the acrobatic display gave me a twinge of rheumatism. Vintage car rally? Lead in the petrol might give us brain-damage. Marineland? We're against dolphins jumping through hoops even if they like it. Bingo? Numbers make me dizzy.

'I used to like Punch and Judy,' I said one day.

'Sex and violence,' Sylvie said. 'Worse than *Miami Vice*.'

In the end we did simple things like watching people going to their deaths over the quicksands. Somehow they always managed to catch the next bus back from Grange-over-Sands.

The weather went in fits and starts. Monday, sunny but cool. Tuesday, damp and grey with the beach glistening like an arctic waste. Wednesday, hot enough to grow bananas with the steam rising from Happy Mount Park. Then Thursday, stormy, causing the dancers on the pier to buffet each other as they invented new steps to fit in with the wind. And there was our son of the desert doing the hokey-cokey with one hand, and holding his tea-towel on with the other.

'He's always there wherever we go,' observed Sylvie, sorting out her knitting. 'Hasn't he got enough women at home?'

When the wind dropped we walked up to Hest Bank and on towards Silverdale looking for migratory birds. I took my reporter's notebook with me as we were right on the flight path and I didn't want to miss anything. I owe it to posterity. Numerous species inhabit the nature reserve at Leighton Moss and feed in the bay. We sat for quite some time eating our cheese rolls and individual fruit pies but we never saw anything.

'Look! Isn't that one?' Sylvie kept saying, pointing with her knitting needle.

There was a black speck on the tideline and I sat with my eyes glued on it for fifteen minutes. Had it moved or hadn't it? No it hadn't.

'It's not moving,' I informed Madame Defarge.

'P'raps it's dead,' she said.

I shook my head to uncross my eyes as I reached for my notebook. 'One dead bird left behind in the migration,' I wrote. 'Conditions unfavourable for twitching.' Presently it began to rain and Sylvie was afraid of getting her knitting wet so we unrolled our plastic macs and made our way back, looking like a couple of walking concertinas.

'What's that?' Sylvie asked, as a stone came rolling down the cliff towards us. I looked up and there was somebody spying on us through a pair of binoculars.

'If it's that Arab again I'm going to the police station,' Sylvie said, gritting her teeth. 'Look, he's following us.'

I turned round in time to catch a glimpse of a red-and-white checked tea-towel dodge behind a tree. There's some weirdos about these days.

'I hope you like Turkish Delight.' I giggled.

'I prefer Walnut Whips,' Sylvie said, after giving it some thought.

We fell to wondering what it would be like in his harem. Sherbet dabs, sugared almonds, jasmine tea, and diamonds to put in your belly-button. Can't be bad, I thought, looking at the cubic zirconia in my belated engagement ring. You all help each other, do your good deed for the day and do what the pack leader says.

'It's like being in the Brownies,' I said.

'I don't fancy eating sheeps' eyes, though,' said Sylvie shuddering. 'Like jelly aniseed-balls.'

'They'll be insulted if you don't eat them,' I told her. 'They'll tie you up in a sack and throw you in the Bosphorus.'

In the end we decided not to go. I remembered the time that I had to prepare a sheep's head for Otley when we were first married. Granny Hawkweed used to do them with onions and carrots, and put the brains on a saucer with pepper on. I didn't fancy it, being a vegetarian, but he threatened to strangle me if I didn't get one, so I scoured all the offal shops in the vicinity until I found one. All the dogs in the neighbourhood followed me home and stood yapping at the garden gate.

I put it in a big pot with some Oxo cubes and soon it was gurgling away as if it were still alive. Every time I lifted the lid to see how it was getting on it grinned at me and moved its mouth as if it were singing. To cut a long story short, when Otley came home he found me in a dead faint on the kitchen floor. He promised to stick to tripe and onions after that. Eating eye-balls would be a similar experience.

'Look! He's running round that way,' Sylvie said, pointing to a path leading into a little copse. 'If he comes out by that gate we can catch him and trip him up.'

She held her knitting needle like a dagger and I brandished my Thermos flask as we hid behind a holly bush. We could say to the learned judge, 'We were peacefully picnicking in the woods, your Honour, when this savage beast leapt upon us.' We threw some twigs of holly down across the path as we heard him approaching. The tea-towel and the dark glasses came into view first as he came creeping along; then a hawk nose over a black beard and moustache as he stood up to his full height, then a bellow of rage as his sandalled feet met the prickly holly.

I darted out and hit him on the head with the Thermos, knocking him down, while Sylvie pinned his head-dress to the ground with the knitting needle. In the struggle to get up the whole lot came away – tea-towel, glasses, false nose and beard.

'You stupid sods, you nearly killed me!' Otley complained, as he pulled the prickles out of his socks.

'You!' I exclaimed in disbelief.

'There's no need to resort to violence,' he said, rubbing his head.

'We thought it was Omar Sharif collecting for his harem,' Sylvie said.

'What would he want with you two silly buggers?' he said.

'What's the idea?' I said crossly. 'I'll have to get a new Thermos now, all because of you.' The flask rattled ominously as I shook it.

'And you've bent my knitting needle,' Sylvie wailed. 'I can't knit round corners.'

'The doctor said I had to keep an eye on you, didn't he?' Otley said. 'I'm responsible for you – I don't want blaming if you go shop-lifting in Marks & Spencers.'

'Anyway, where's Bella?' I asked him. 'I hope you haven't left her on her own when she's highly strung.'

'She's gone to Butlins with Crispin,' he jeered.

'With Crispin?' I echoed.

'Yes, Crispin,' he repeated. 'Your bloody fancy-man.'

'What for?' I couldn't help wondering where Gordon was.

'She's keeping him out of the way to give us a chance to make up; how's that for self-sacrifice?' he said reverently.

'That's nice of her,' Sylvie said.

'Don't worry about us,' I told him. 'We've had a few days' rest and a bit of sea breeze; we're going back tomorrow.'

'I'll come back with you,' he volunteered.

'I'm all right; you stay if you want to,' I assured him.

'I must say, you've been behaving a lot better since you started taking those tablets,' he said, patting me on the back like a pet poodle.

'I'm not taking them – I threw 'em down the lavatory,' I said.

There was a shocked silence and then he reminded me how much they cost.

'You could have given 'em to me couldn't you? Selfish madam.'

We tidied ourselves up and Otley rescued the Groucho Marx nose and moustache that he got from a joke shop, now lying squashed beside his false beard and tattered tea-towel. It was one of my new ones too. He limped along, stopping now and again to examine his feet for prickles. The famous Morecambe sunset reflected in a molten sea, setting the hills ablaze like a necklace of fire-opals. Otley said he would sleep outdoors in his sleeping-bag. No sissy stuff for him. He was to meet us the next day for a last look round before going home.

'I've not been on the Big Wheel yet,' Sylvie complained.

Otley's Hawkweed blood was stirred. We couldn't go without seeing the fairground. Bring back happy memories, wouldn't it? Did I remember the time when we went in the river caves at Blackpool? The boat was leaking and when we got out, my new, blue crêpe frock had shrunk up to my waist and I had to wear his Uncle Joe's old grandad shirt. Then there was a thunderstorm and we sat in a shelter drinking Bovril for the rest of the day. What a laff! When the rain stopped we took some snaps on the sands and they came out looking as if we were at the North Pole standing on a sheet of ice – Auntie Mabel in a fur hat and Uncle Joe in a flat cap and a tweed overcoat.

'See you tomorrow, then,' I said, interrupting his train of thought.

Now I had my Earthman back again he'd be wanting his buttons sewn on as soon as we got home. I gazed up at the Moon, which looked like a slice of melon facing east. How I longed to see my silver man!

'I wonder what Jeff's doing,' I said, half to myself.

'He said he was keeping an eye on Sellafield,' Sylvie told me.

'That's only just up the road,' I said. 'Wouldn't it be fun if he dropped in and took us for a ride?'

'Oh! I don't know about that. There's not much room on the Moon tonight by the looks of it,' Sylvie said, giving it a worried glance.

I looked closer at it. Was that a man hanging on one of its horns, trying to get back on? No, it was only one of the lights dangling on a wire put up for the forthcoming illuminations.

'I'm knitting him a Doctor Who scarf, you know,' Sylvie informed me. 'He says it gets cold at nights.'

'They don't wear scarves – too dangerous. Get caught in the works,' I said. 'They wear body-stockings made out of kitchen foil to keep the heat in.'

'Kitchen foil? Never!' Sylvie tut-tutted.

'Like they wrap them up in at the London Marathon,' I explained.

'What, like a chicken ready for the oven?' she asked in disbelief.

'Like they tell you at Help the Aged – woolly vest, wrap up in a foil blanket with your feet in a fur-lined muff,' I told her.

'Supposing the telephone rings, then?' she wanted to know.

'You fall flat on your face,' I said.

SATURDAY DAWNED WITH
a gentle pearl-grey mist rolling in from the sea; then enough
sun to put a glint on the water, and enough of a breeze to
blow away the heat. Weren't we lucky? Those poor people in
Greece! We said goodbye to the snapdragons on the promenade, and Sylvie and Otley stopped at the oyster bar for
some cockles and whelks. I stood with my back to them and
my fingers in my ears so that I couldn't hear the swallocking.
Then they slurped some oysters. The Roman Empire was
built on oysters, Otley said; and the Vikings went rampaging
on them. He has an oyster-shell at home that he got from the
Viking dig in York. Carelessly cast aside by a Viking chief at
his wedding breakfast, he said, when Eric Bloodaxe made
York the capital of the Viking Empire. Otley still has a T-
shirt saying 'Bloodaxe Rules OK' and a jigsaw of a Viking
longship. But how does he know where the oyster-shell came
from? He's only guessing. It might have been a mangy cur
that ran off with it, or a scruffy Saxon serf that dropped it out
of his bucket of pig-swill. And then again . . .

'You can open your eyes now, we've finished,' Otley announced, with vinegar running down his chin.

'You are silly,' Sylvie told me. 'They're good for you.'

'Lots of iodine in them,' Otley went on.

'I take seaweed tablets, they're not as slimy,' I told them.

Then we had some candy-floss in the fairground and had our photos taken in the stocks. Sylvie was sick in the Ghost Train so we sat down with a cup of tea until she'd recovered enough to go on the Big Wheel. I've got no head for heights so I looked after the bags until they came down again.

'Oh! look, flying saucers!' Sylvie squealed, pointing to some multicoloured discs whizzing round above our heads. They floated by, gliding to a gradual halt: red, blue, yellow, green, and finally a silver one. Someone must have run out of paint. Sylvie and Otley got into a blue flying saucer and beckoned to me.

'Can't get in with them bags,' the attendant cautioned.

'I'll wait here again,' I called out, as they started to move. After much creaking and grinding, whizzing and whirring, they were off. After a while the screaming stopped and the saucers came to rest.

'Hurry up! Get in,' Sylvie urged. 'We'll look after the luggage.'

'I shall get migraine . . .' I began.

'There's a smashing view over the Lake District,' Otley said, pushing me on to the platform. The saucers were beginning to move again. A red one, a green one, a yellow one. They started to pick up speed and just as I was turning away a large hand propelled me into the silver one.

'Get in if you're going,' the attendant snapped.

I picked myself up off the floor and looked out to give Sylvie and Otley a wave but there was no sign of them. Where was everybody? And the yellow saucer in front had gone. This would have to be reported to the safety inspectorate. Somebody not doing their job.

Then I noticed the port-holes round the side. Just like the Earthskimmer. I looked out of the nearest one and saw the Isle of Man dwindling rapidly into a dot. Then the jagged inlets and islands of the west coast of Scotland, scattered like the pieces of a jigsaw waiting to be put together again. There was a rustling noise like somebody eating chocolates.

'Is that you, Jeff?' I called.

A panel slid open and two figures appeared dressed in iridescent skin-tight suits. I looked closer. It was Bella and Steve Hurst.

'I thought you were at Butlins,' I said, when I had got over my astonishment.

'Bella's come for the weekend,' Steve explained. 'If she likes it I'm bringing Gordon as well; my people are leaderless and godless, at war with the Selenites.'

'What's that got to do with me?' I asked.

'We want a mediator,' he went on. 'Something like ACAS; the Selenites don't trust us and we don't trust them.' He looked different somehow, his face had a gilded appearance, like an ormolu clock.

'And they want somebody plain and simple to record their dynastic history,' Bella said. 'You know, they don't want the men losing their marbles.' She had a golden cobra round her neck with emerald eyes and a forked tongue spitting rubies. Her black hair snaked down her back in Medusa locks. She'd go down a treat at the Rose & Crown.

'I have to do my diary,' I told them.

'It would only be for two months or so, till we've got things sorted out; we're fed up of Earth – all the aggro and the filth,' Steve said.

'Are you deserting us, then?' I inquired fearfully.

'We'll still be around, keeping an eye on things, and we'll drop in occasionally,' he said, pointing to a wall-map with lights flashing on and off. 'Jeff's doing the nuclear accidents and we're doing the chemical stuff.'

Seveso, Bhopal, Flixborough, Rhine, Ganges, said the map as it changed minute by minute. Below us the lush, green Amazonian rainforest came into view, gashed by ugly brown scars as more and more trees are murdered.

'One day it'll be like the Sahara,' Steve said.

'I'll help if you'll promise me something,' I told him.

'What's that, then?' he inquired.

'Don't tell my husband what I did with the rats,' I begged.

'Is that all?' he wanted to know.

'Just tell him they've gone to a good home in Halifax,' I said.

'Of course. I'm very grateful to you, Gordon enjoyed them,' he assured me, as if they were cucumber sandwiches.

'My husband would murder me if he knew,' I said frantically.

'It's a deal,' he said.

'I can't stay long, I'll just come and see where you live this time,' I said, looking down at my crumpled pac-a-mac. 'If you let me know when you're going to pick me up I can put something decent on.'

'Jeff'll arrange that when you see him,' Bella put in hastily.

Soon Earth was a shining blue-green-silver bauble in the black and velvet sky and we were putting down in the fine, grey Moondust.

'This is the Mare Nectaris,' Steve said, when the door slid open, 'the other side of the moon from the Selenites.'

We got into our jumping suits and bounded away towards a blaze of light in the distance. Sound was muffled as at the bottom of a swimming pool.

The Serpent People, small and dark, left their home star when the air became too poisonous to breathe. Some went down to Earth and hid in the hot, steaming jungles with the snakes. Some stayed on the moon.

We entered a large glass dome, like the hot-house at Kew, pausing in an ante-room to change into sarongs and sip lemonade. Giant ferns and orchids grew beside a lagoon; I trailed my hand in the water, feeling like Dorothy Lamour in *The Jungle Princess*.

'It's nice. I don't know why you wanted to go to Butlins,' I said.

'There is hidden sadness,' Steve said. 'When The Wise One is restored all will be as it was in the beginning.'

'The Wise One?' I asked.

'Our serpent god,' he replied.

'D'you mean Gordon?' I inquired, thinking of him wriggling about in that zipped-up canvas bag. Was it a portable altar as used by the Pope?

'The same,' Steve went on, 'and he never forgets a friend; that day you gave me the rats he'd . . .' He choked on the words and his eyes filled with tears.

'He'd what?' I asked, dabbing his eyes with the corner of my sarong.

'Well,' he said, 'he'd had nothing but Whiskas and Kattomeat for the past six weeks.'

'I'm so glad Mickey and Minnie were able to be of some use,' I said, as if they had been helping out with 'Bob a Job' week.

Bella looked ravishing in an iridescent gown shining turquoise blue and silver, like a butterfly's wings. Peacock feathers in her hair and bright, jewelled humming-birds in her ears.

'They'll love you,' her spaceman cried. 'You'll be a fine queen.'

'Not bad for a tinker's brat, is it?' she whispered to me.

Later on Steve introduced her to his people and prepared them for the return of The Wise One. Then he pulled me forward.

'And this is the plain she from Earth who is to record our

history before it vanishes for ever in the mists of time,' he announced.

There was a rumble of discontent and I felt silly standing there holding a Marks & Spencer's carrier with a change of underwear in it. How had I got myself into this mess? What if Sylvie and Otley were still waiting there in the fairground? What if Mike and Heron went to San Francisco before I got back? What if the house burnt down? I couldn't remember whether I'd turned the gas off or not. The magistrate would say, 'This foolish woman went gallivanting off to the moon and left her husband to get his own dinner.' Then again I might be given a Dameship.

'If you're sure there's nobody else to do it . . .' I began.

'You've got the magic pen that cannot be rubbed out,' Steve said.

'Well, you've got a computer, haven't you?' I said hopefully.

'It's always up the creek,' he said.

'Oh, all right, then,' I said, 'I'll do it.'

I promised to put in a good word for them with the Selenites. They wanted to pool their resources and have an exchange of information. Research was being duplicated, wasting time and money. They'd both brought an elephant back when one would have been enough; there were too many rabbits and they could do with some John Innes potting compost.

'They didn't seem to like the idea of me doing the records,' I said to Steve, as we went to look for a Kraak to jump me over to Jeff.

'Only the elders know our history. They pass it on by word of mouth, like your Druids; he who holds a secret, holds power,' he explained.

'I'll do it nice,' I said, anxious to please. 'If you want pictures in it like the Lindisfarne Gospels . . .'

'Can you do that?' he said admiringly.

'Well, not really.' What had I said? 'But I can do feathers and ladybirds . . .'

'Just stick to the facts,' he said sternly.

The Kraak seemed pleased to see me and I held on to his wing as we leapt over the mountains to the other side of the moon. The Great Dome of Selenus lay low in the crater like a half-buried turtle's egg. We came to land on the viewing platform and slid helter-skelter-wise to the bottom, tumbling into the brightly lit piazza. The Kraak lumbered awkwardly to his feathered feet. I took off my goldfish bowl.

'Take me to your leader,' I said.

The sun's rays slanted in through the glass turning Jeff to silver-gold, like one of those old EPNS spoons with the gilt coming through.

'You'll be pleased to know that the pound has fallen only half a cent against the dollar,' he said, listening to his new Russian Super Snooper Radio that he had sent for out of the daily paper.

'It's ages since I saw you . . .' I began.

'And Ronnie and Gorby are getting together on the IBM treaty at last,' he said, delighted with his new toy.

I moved closer and locked into his magnetic field. I ran my fingers up and down his spine. He still had no knobs on; I don't know what holds him up. One good thump and I'd find out if he rattled like a money-box, but I couldn't bring myself to do it. Supposing all the little wheels fell out and he lay whirring like a clockwork toy with the spring broken. I'd never forgive myself. I waited until he switched off his Super Snooper and got to his feet. I looked into his eyes desperate to see the end of the video where we'd left off in the conservatory. We were star-hopping through the Milky Way; Jeff was driving with his feet as he had both hands occupied in programming the computer; Kraak was playing the pan-pipes that his cousin Colin Condor sent him from the Andes. I was knitting a silver dish-cloth.

'Are you all right, Mrs Craven?' Jeff inquired.

'When are you coming down to High Riding again?' I asked him. 'The morris men are getting restless – nothing to do but pick caterpillars off the cabbages.'

'I'll be back for the bank holiday and the fertility dance,' he said, 'and I want to see if Thelma's got any painted ladies and holly blues.'

I delivered Steve's message and he said it sounded interesting and he would arrange a summit meeting. Nothing in a hurry, though; he might set up a Royal Commission to look into it. The Selenites didn't trust the Serpents. Can't change the habits of a lifetime overnight.

'They were pretty decent to me,' I told him. 'Just because their eyes slant up!'

I thought he might have missed me but it seemed he'd been too busy generating since I last saw him. He showed me round the nursery and there were rows of cocoons hanging by a silver thread like silk-worms.

'That's Mick, that's Nigel, this is Wayne, Sharron, Tracy, Clint, Burt and Cynthia; and this is Beryl – she'll be hatching any minute,' he said, as we went along the line. I touched one and it squeaked.

'Dear little things, aren't they?' I said conversationally. 'When will they learn to play the fiddle?'

When could we book our places up here? Jeff wanted to know. We hadn't much time left according to Nostradamus and Old Mother Shipton – either we would poison ourselves or blow ourselves up!

'We'll keep our options open,' I told him. The Moon was nice but it wasn't like walking through the heather on Ilkley Moor.

'First come, first served,' he said.

The dome began to move out of the crater and we climbed up to the viewing platform. Jeff put his arm round me and I was held as if in a vice, clamped to his side like a pin picked up by a magnet.

'If we could go in the rejuvenator and start again it might be worth thinking about,' I told him. I had a fleeting glimpse of Mike as a silk cocoon. He would be easier to deal with that way. One squeak and it would be a simple matter to unravel him.

A million stars shone with a steady glow sprinkling the night with gold-dust. Earth hanging low in the sky lighting up the distant ranges and seeming to deposit them at our feet. White mountains and black shadows. A surrealist dreamscape. Stark, breathless and dead. Poor old Earth, we can't let her die too. We watched the sun's corona set the sky ablaze then skeltered down to the piazza before turning in for the night. I've got to get back tomorrow; my husband will be looking for his clean socks.

I didn't like the way Elin looked at me when we went in to supper. Like a cat that's run off with a kipper. She sat between me and Jeff and gave him all the best tit-bits. All I had were some of those floury crispbreads that taste like dusty, old shoe-boxes and a piece of stale cheese. I slipped it into my plastic bag to make a poverty pie with when I got home.

'Which tea would you like?' inquired the acolyte standing by. 'Earl Grey or Lapsang-Souchong; Orange Pekoe or Darjeeling?'

'Have you got any Co-op 99?' I inquired. It was Granny's favourite.

'I'm afraid it hasn't come our way,' Elin replied.

'I'll bring you some next time I come up,' I told her.

'Don't bother!' she said.

The fare was very Spartan, just the basics: bread, cheese, textured vegetable protein and packets of instant potato the Selenites had brought up from Morrisons; jam and fish-paste, rice and dried peas and beans. They were having a load of manure delivered and some young saplings to plant. The more trees they could grow, the more fertile the soil would become, enabling them to grow fresh vegetables. Until then they took vitamin pills and meditated standing on their heads to take away the hunger pangs.

'The Serpents have got bananas and lemonade,' I told Jeff later as I was shown to my cell.

'Have they?' he said. 'I'll dispense with the Royal Commission and bring the Summit Meeting forward to next week.'

'I'd like to sleep in the bluebell wood tonight, if I can,' I said to him. 'I suffer from claustrophobia.' This wasn't the cosy little room I had last time. It was more like a urinal, all gleaming porcelain.

'There's only the hammock. I'll show you where it is,' he said, leading me past the music room where somebody was scraping away making a noise like a circular saw cutting through rusty, old iron railings. I expect they've all got tin ears in these parts.

I tried to get into the hammock but fell over the other side. I caught it again as it swung to and fro above my head. I then threw my left leg at it and grabbed it with both hands, but it slipped out of my grasp and I found myself swinging by one leg like a pendulum. I grabbed hold of the tree and came to a halt. The only thing was to climb up it and slide into the hammock from the branch it was tied to. Luckily it held but I landed face down and it took me some time to get the right way up.

Earth shone through the honeycombed glass multiplying itself into a thousand Chinese lanterns. I wondered if Otley was waiting for me in Morecambe, or if he had gone home to test the pauper's pottage for milliSieverts. Please God let him put hemlock in it instead of cow-parsley.

THE SCENT OF bluebells all around made me feel homesick and I decided to take the first saucer back. Getting out of a hammock is easier than getting in, you just fall out sideways as if you had a slipped disc. The sky was still as black as midnight and Earth seemed hardly to have moved. The woodland path led out into the kitchen garden where the Selenites were busy tending rows of scrawny lettuces and runner beans. You can pick better ones out of the gutter down the market. My Earth! If only I were back home wokking!

Elin was waiting in the office with my jumping-suit and goldfish bowl. Smiling that secret smile. Were those things cocoons she had in that big pocket at the front of her blue kangaroo suit?

'It's been nice having you,' she murmured, as she pulled the cord around my neck a little too tight. I gurgled a bit and released it.

'My pleasure,' I managed to say.

Jeff was at the airport checking the skimmers and he

stowed me into Recorder Five. The Kraak got in after me and began testing the control panel. I put my shopping bag down and went to the door to say goodbye to Jeff; he put his arms round me and his eyes sparkled in the Earthlight like the star sapphire in Princess Di's engagement ring.

'Don't forget bank holiday?' he said.

'I won't,' I told him.

'Have your bags packed ready for a long stay.'

'I will, I will.'

'And keep your eye on the heather on Ilkley Moor,' he went on. 'It's getting trampled to death.'

'I know, they don't care.'

'Cheerio, then,' he said, 'and don't do anything I wouldn't do.'

'I can't,' I said.

I tried to break away but in the end it took a violent push to send me back into the skimmer. The door closed, there was a mighty whoosh! and we were airborne. Kraak was collecting samples of cotton-grass and bog asphodel up on the high moors, but he could drop me by the canal towpath, near Dingle Bottoms, where the tinkers live.

'Good boy,' I said, stroking his feathers.

I looked out of the port-hole to see the Moon falling away like a beach-ball tossed on the waves. Earth shone in the blackness clear as a jewel in a blackamoor's navel, but soon we encountered the sulphurous fumes spewed out by the string of power stations. We were home! Below the level of the chimneys the air was clear, the landing lights came on and we fell gently like an autumn leaf. I gave the Kraak a piece of paper with my measurements on and was about to ask him for a feather when I suddenly found myself in the canal, while the saucer skimmed the tree-tops away over Hawkcliff Wood.

I hauled myself up on to the *River Queen* and sat picking the pondweed out of my hair. It was just cracking dawn with the sun a bold brass gong on the horizon. The humming of a thousand washing machines told me it was Monday. Good job my reporter's notebook was in its plastic envelope.

10 August 2 AC

The purple bellflower stoops like the Archbishop of Canterbury blessing his flock. The spotted burnets are on the wing, little flying dominoes. Crispin to the aid of a poor, benighted farmer who needs must bury his cattle as they do not conform to Common Market regulations. A little water-skater skims the surface doing triple toe-loops, breaks his legs and is eaten by Freddie Frog.

> Poor Bobby Beetle, gone from the scene,
> He wasn't as good as Torvill and Dean.

My beloved carried home in a dung-cart under cover of darkness. I fear he hath been stricken with the rinderpest. He is now bedded in the stable, his rhubarb refresher by his side ere he awakes. My ill-starred love!

A wisp of blue smoke rose from Dingle Bottoms – that would be the tinkers; perhaps they could give me a lift home. I followed the smell of bacon and eggs and axle-grease into a clearing in the copse. An old railway carriage with LMS on the side lay in the undergrowth, sacks up at the broken windows, the door hanging like a drunken sailor to a taffrail. A shotgun appeared as if by magic followed by a grizzled head wearing a battered felt hat.

'If tha's come for t'poll tax tha can bugger off – am not payin' it,' he said, aiming the gun between my eyes.

'It's Mrs Craven,' I said, introducing myself.

'Bugger off!' he said.

'I fell in the canal,' I explained, 'and I wondered if you could give me a lift home.' He seemed to be wavering and I played an ace. 'I'll pay you,' I said, as he lowered the gun to my innards ready to disembowel me.

'American Express?' he inquired.

'Er . . . well, no,' I confessed, 'but I've got a budget account with the Co-op.'

'What's that, then?' he wanted to know, not taking any chances.

'Well, it's handy if you want a new food-mixer, or . . .' I began.

'We don't 'ave food long enough to mix it,' he said.

'You can get anything you want,' I said recklessly.

'Can yer get a record o' 'Arry Champion singin' "Any Old Iron"?' he inquired, after giving it some thought.

'No,' I had to say.

'No good to me, then,' he decided.

I promised to give him a £5 note when I got home. I must have been mad, the bus fare's only thirty pence off-peak, but I was desperate. I couldn't get on the bus in the state I was in – hair like dreadlocks, mud-plastered jeans and shoes squelching with pondweed.

'Ira's out rabbitin' and Swire's taken t' wagon lookin' fer railway sleepers . . .' He stopped to pick his teeth and think.

'Yes?' I said.

'Seth's gone 'arvestin', Job's up in t' quarry and Jabus 'as taken t' motor for ta fetch a fly-wheel for t' steam-roller.'

'And?'

'Yer'll 'ave ter take t' owd 'oss,' he said.

He vanished into the bushes and appeared again leading a skewbald, sickle-hocked, mongrel moke. I'd never ridden before and there was no saddle. In for a penny, in for a pound. Once I was aboard I felt like Belle Starr, Queen of the West. Had it been up to High Riding before?

'She knows t' way; goes up there every Friday rag an' bonein'.'

'Who's going to bring her back?' I asked anxiously.

'Just give 'er a smack an' she'll be off like the divil,' he said.

'Oh, all right.'

'Don't let 'er drink too much – she'll get belly-ache,' he went on.

'I won't.'

'An' if she stops, kick 'er in the guts an' get 'er goin' again.'

'Cheerio and thanks,' I called as we clip-clopped into a pleasant country lane. 'What's her name?'

'Dandy – if we call her owt.'

We took a short-cut, following the bridle-path through the woods and up on to the moor. I didn't want anyone to see me. The sun came dappling through the trees, waking up the honeysuckle and the songbirds. Hedgerows tumbling with rose hips, bindweed and enchanter's nightshade. It was a lot better than the Moon.

Dandy stopped to drink at a murky ditch. I didn't want her to get typhoid so I pulled at her mane to try and get her head up. She pulled back and I was left holding a bunch of horsehair.

'Gee up!' I said.

When she had drunk her fill and cropped the grass all round we moved off again, emerging into the open at the head of the valley; a gentle boulder-strewn slope down, then a pleasant ride up through the heather and we would be home. Olé!

Dandy called first at a clump of blackberry bushes and chompled a few.

'Gee up!' I said.

She looked at the boulders and then tossed her head as much as to say, 'I'm not going down there.'

'Gee up!' I said again.

She bit off a twig of hawthorn with its fresh, juicy leaves and stuck it in the corner of her mouth to eat later.

'Gee up!' I said.

She took no notice so I gave her a sharp dig in the ribs with my heels; in a trice we were galloping like mad down the hill, heading for a large lump of millstone grit lying in wait half-way down.

'Whoa! Whoa there!' I shouted.

I felt myself slipping off and put my arms round her neck, but she was enjoying herself now. Slowly I slid off her back and under her belly; she was beginning to slow down and I hung on to her neck with one leg on her back and the other trailing on the ground.

'Whoa! there, good girl,' I said, getting a mouthful of mane.

When she was ready she stopped, still with the twig in her mouth, as nonchalant as Noël Coward with a cigarette-holder. I hauled myself on to her back and we proceeded up through the heather at a more sedate pace. I was too tired to dismount and breathe up her nostrils like Barbara Woodhouse, but all told I could have walked it more quickly.

Soon we were at High Riding and I planned to sneak round the back of the wilderness and tidy myself up in the Big House before Otley saw me but he was testing the cabbages for milliSieverts and heard us clip-clopping up the drive. You'd have thought I was Lady Godiva the way he stared.

'Good God! Where have you been to?' he demanded.

'I've been to the Moon,' I said, pointing up at the sky.

'What, on a bloody horse?' he said.

'No – on a flying saucer,' I said. 'They dropped me in the canal.'

He dragged me off Dandy's back and she trotted off, whinnying with pleasure. His eyes were swivelling so I thought I'd better take his mind off the subject. Talk about something he was interested in.

'What's the level of background radiation these days?' I inquired.

'Is that all you've got to say for yourself?' he stormed. 'I've had no Sunday dinner, spent all Saturday afternoon wandering round Morecambe looking for you and all you're bothered about is bloody radiation!'

'Stop shouting. I've got a splitting headache,' I moaned.

'That's your guilty conscience,' he told me.

Suddenly I felt very tired. My legs were bruised where they had hit the millstone grit and I was suffering from culture shock – flying saucer to one-horse-power at the speed of light. Otley caught me as I crumpled and sat me down among the weeds. A cloud of white butterflies rose from the organic cabbages; a flutter of bright tortoiseshells flirted with a clump of nettles; a bumble-bee buzzed happily in and out of sweet-scented nasturtiums living inside an old car tyre; the sun beat down and the heat was carried away on a gentle breeze. I took a deep breath and closed my eyes.

'Are you all right?' Otley asked, with a note of faint concern.

'Just bring me a cup of tea and two aspirins and I'm in paradise,' I said, as I inhaled the perfume of a piece of crushed pineapple weed.

Later on I cleaned up the cottage, flinging all the doors and windows open to get rid of the peculiar smell. My life has consisted mostly of cleaning up dirt. It's the only thing I've got against Earth. Soon everything was dinky again and the *Thousand and One Nights* odour was replaced by a fresh bluster blowing in off the moor.

Bob Hope said we had four seasons to the day in the British Isles. Well, we get four to the hour here on the edge of the Pennines. The hurricane whistles through the Aire Gap, picks up the whinook on Haworth Moor, then swirls it over to Ilkley Moor and back again. Sun, rain, sun, sleet – you can't put your umbrella up and down quickly enough to keep up with it. You go out walking equipped for an arctic expedition and suddenly it's hot, and the water sparkling blue like a holiday brochure. Makes you want to spit.

'What's for dinner?' the master called as I was having a lie down.

Trossachs! I thought, pretending to be asleep. After a while he brought me a cup of tea and I was obliged to get up.

'You're going to end up in a padded cell if you go on the way you are doing,' he cautioned. It looked as if he did care about me after all. His eyes had lost their glass-marble glint and took on the soft green of a forest floor.

'You said I could go if I wanted,' I reminded him, 'and Jeff's been very helpful, explaining everything.'

'Well, I've changed my mind,' he said. 'If you go up there again I shall see my solicitor.'

'All right,' I said.

'Promise?' he asked, putting his hand on the place where his heart used to be. 'Finger wet, finger dry, cross my heart if I tell a lie?'

'Honest,' I lied, and then put my hand on my heart afterwards. I now had two promises to keep. I must help them on the Moon, poor souls, living up there among all that dust. It won't hurt to tell Otley a white lie; I can tell him I'm washing up at Butlins so I can buy him a new telescope for his birthday.

'What's for dinner?' he inquired. 'I'm fed up of bloody bamboo shoots.'

'I've got some stale cheese here; I can make a poverty pie now,' I said triumphantly as I shook out the contents of my carrier-bag, still tied to my jeans with a piece of string. Out tumbled the cheese along with damp underwear and

187

nightgown containing water-beetles, pondweed and squashed marsh marigolds.

'What's this?' he demanded, as my notebook and pencil fell out of a pair of knickers. He riffled quickly through the pages and his face turned as purple as a cardinal's cassock.

'Nothing,' I said, snatching it from him.

'I knew it! You've been with that bloody Crispin again,' he raged.

'I haven't, I haven't,' I said. 'It's all in the mind . . .'

'And don't give me that guff about bloody Martin Chuzzlewit again, either,' he continued, snatching it back out of my hands.

'Give me it,' I said, grabbing hold of one corner. 'It's private.'

'I'll murder you one of these days, I swear I will,' he said, giving my hand a karate chop. I let go.

'Wait till I've deposited my diary in the archives,' I pleaded. 'You owe it to posterity.'

'Bugger posterity,' he said. 'He doesn't care about me.'

We tussled and grappled with each other while the notebook lay on the floor watching us. I reached for it and he stood on my hand.

'You clog-dancing baldric,' I screamed. 'You poncing poltroon, you bogswalloping beadle, you . . .'

'I didn't know you cared,' he smirked, kicking my notebook into touch.

In the films they say 'Darling, you're lovely when you're angry.' I rescued my battered treasure and hid it under the mattress as he went downstairs.

'Hurry up,' he called, 'or we'll miss *Wogan*.'

I don't know what I shall do on the Moon; they've got no television up there yet. You can't be generating all the time and I can't play the violin – Granny bought me one when I was seven but I put it in a bucket of whitewash when she wasn't looking.

The poverty pie came out nicely though I say it myself; a salad of grated carrot, Good King Henry, and nasturtium leaves went with it.

'I hope you got all the blackfly off it,' Otley grumbled.

Stewed apple made with windfalls, home-made yoghurt and a pot of local heather honey, which we got in exchange for two pots of marrow and ginger jam. Once you get the hang of this do-it-yourself thing it's not bad; only I'm not going to make raffia table-mats for anybody.

We watched the 'talking heads' with their thumbs up. Then another version of *The Godfather*, which brought us up to the ten o'clock news. Ronnie – Gorby – Maggie – Walid Jumblatt – Tamil Tigers – Sandanistas – Mudjahadeen – Gaza Strip . . . I was just nodding off when Otley roused me and gave me a glass of nettle beer.

'D'you hear that?' he said excitedly.

It seems the EEC has started legal proceedings against the British government for failing to bring its drinking water up to safer levels.

'Good for them!' I exclaimed.

Sometimes when it rains heavily we get brown water and they tell us it's only peat off the moors and it's quite safe to drink. It could be sewage, for all we know.

'Glad we joined the Common Market now, we shall soon be Europeans,' Otley said. It's the first time I've heard him say that.

Tornado in Edmonton – floods in Nepal – famine in Ethiopia again – Bank of England base rate up by one per cent – can't read *Spycatcher* – dear oh dear! What is to become of our poor old planet? All we can do is our little best and pray hard. I closed my eyes and began to murmur my own special incantation,

'Rockall, Dogger, German Bight . . .'

'Stop swearing,' Otley said, giving me a dig in the ribs.

'That wasn't Crispin at the hospital, that was Steve Hurst,' I told Otley for the umpteenth time the next morning.

'Him who took the rats?' he inquired.

'You remember,' I nodded. 'Lives on the council estate. They came from Serpentis originally.'

'You're as mad as a hatter,' he said, after a minute's silence.

'Only by marriage,' I said, dodging out of the way.

'Bella's gone away with him for my sake,' he went on. 'Sacrificing herself like Mrs Simpson did when she fled to the continent; she does not want me to abdicate my responsibilities.'

'What responsibilities?' I asked.

'There's the Neighbourhood Watch,' he said. 'And I can't desert you now when everybody knows you're off your rocker.'

'Bella's on the Moon anyway,' I told him. 'She's going to be Queen of the Serpent people.'

He looked startled and then patted me on the head, offering to do the washing-up. He'd do the shopping as well if I liked and pop down the village to see Mike. He's a saint, really.

'They'll be back for the bank-holiday do and then we'll see who's lying,' he said giving me an old-fashioned look.

It was thelma's idea to have a garden party at High Riding in aid of the World Wildlife Fund. She had murdered so many butterflies on her rampages in foreign parts that she now wanted to make up for it in some way. There would be the morris dancers and three-legged races in the afternoon; sack races and side-shows; open-air dancing and musical entertainment in the evening. Sylvie would be doing a selection from *The King and I* with Sammy Chandra's extended family as the supporting cast. Mike was all set to give 'Silver Riding' its world première.

'Jeff'll be coming down for the morris dancing,' I assured Otley.

'Look,' he said, 'if you mention bloody flying saucers once more I'll have you certified.'

'It was you who mentioned them in the first place,' I said. 'And everybody's seen them whizzing about – they're well documented.'

'It's a different matter seeing 'em to saying you've been up in one,' he said, getting exasperated.

'A matter of degree, that's all,' I said, trying to look intelligent.

'All right, Madame Curie, get on with your knitting and don't talk about things you know nothing about,' he said loftily.

'I don't know anything about buses either but I've been on one,' I said. 'And I know most of the drivers – they always give me a wave.'

'I expect they're sorry for you,' he said.

'It's nice up there on the Moon,' I said, trying to put him in a good mood. 'You want to go for an awayday sometime.'

'With my free bus pass and a bottle o' pop?' he sniggered.

'They have a message for us: we're destroying our spaceship Earth and there won't be enough room for us all up there,' I told him.

'Don't go broadcasting it all over the place, then,' he said.

'That reminds me, I'm on Radio Leeds next week,' I announced.

'It's asking for trouble to go there talking about flying saucers,' he said, as if to a half-witted, blue-footed booby.

'Why is it?' I asked. 'They only want to know how it feels.'

'It's like religion,' he went on. 'You can believe in God without saying you had a pint with him round the pub.'

I followed him when he went out shopping in case he was going to order the funny-farm wagon. The sun shone after the rain making the valley below steam like a tropical rainforest. Otley was nowhere in sight; he must have taken the short cut through Boggle's field on a fungus foray. Please God, I prayed silently, let him pick fly agaric thinking it's a fairy toadstool and then I won't have to be locked in a padded cell. I touched my Egyptian scarab for luck, it's a wooden one I got from the shop in the British Museum twenty-five years ago. All the hieroglyphics have worn off and it looks like a salted peanut, but there's a chance it might still be working.

My shins were still bruised and I couldn't hope to catch up with a maniac with long legs, so I stopped a double-decker with 'Bradford's Bouncing Back!' all over it.

'Can you put me off at the junction by the old signal-box, I'm not sure where it is?' I asked the driver.

'I don't know where it is either,' he said.

Since deregulation, it's a bit like going on a mystery tour when you get on a bus. You go winding in and out of all the estates and if you're not careful you can end up back where you started from, like the Hampton Court maze. Old Inky Popplewell went down to the Post Office to draw his pension and ended up on Baildon Moor, pensionless.

A public-spirited traveller put me off at the right place and I set off down the disused railway line, jumping from sleeper to sleeper like we used to do coming home from school,

> 'If you tread on a nick
> You'll marry a dick'

we used to chant. Ragwort and rose-bay willow-herb had now taken over from the Puffing Billies. For a minute I forgot I had a bad leg.

No sign of Otley in the supermarket. Hordes of people waiting outside with trolleys full of soap powder, washing-up liquid, bleach and aerosols for sterilizing and polishing every surface known to man. With such a hygiene-conscious population it's a puzzle why everything's so filthy. And the hole in the ozone layer gets bigger every day.

I pressed my nose against the jeweller's shop-window again and then turned away quickly. It's all right if you look like Elizabeth Taylor. Was that somebody hiding behind the telephone-box? He bobbed back just as I looked. If it's my husband with the men from the funny farm I'm not going without a fight. I intend to write to the European Commission of Human Rights; I know what I can say.

'May it please your honours to consider a plaint by one May Craven, Ancient Briton of this parish, whose husband, a football hooligan, is plotting to deprive her of her liberty against the spirit of the 1975 Helsinki agreement. I feel it my duty to warn you that he has applied for a ticket to the European Cup Final and is already in possession of smoke-bombs, toilet-rolls and a rattle. I heartily applaud your fine action in banning English clubs from Europe and would ask you to extend this ban to the United Kingdom. Hoping this finds you as it leaves me at present. SWALK.'

Perhaps Sammy Chandra could tell me what the future holds.

'Mrs Craven!' he exclaimed in answer to my knock. 'It is a long time since I saw you; I thought you were dead.'

I followed him into the parlour, where he spread his charts out on the table. The Benares brass glowed in the light of an imitation oil-lamp; a decapitated rose floated in a saucer of water escorted by a glass fish with rolling eyes, and a trail of breadcrumbs led to a pile of hastily prepared sandwiches.

'How's Mrs Chandra?' I inquired.

His black eyes flashed as he took off his green velvet jacket and donned his forecasting garment of gold lamé, embroidered with lotuses and signs of the zodiac.

'It is a matter of regret that she has taken it upon herself to obtain a Bachelor of Science degree in meteorology, and attends the technical college every day; she gets her onion *bhajis* from Marks & Spencer now.'

'I'm sorry,' I said.

'She might just as well have absconded with her paramour on the Minster & Selby Line,' he said, through gritted teeth.

'And how's the rest of the family, then?' I asked cheerfully.

'They are appearing in *The King and I* and are no doubt showing their legs to the universe; a great disgrace has fallen upon my house.'

'Oh! it's not as bad as all that,' I said rashly.

'They watch *EastEnders* and have fallen into evil ways,' he wailed.

'Never mind, chin up! What have the stars got for me, then?' I said, sick of all this moaning.

'She is totally without scruple,' he grumbled on, 'leaving me to be found dead when the Meals on Wheels lady looks through the letterbox.'

'I didn't know they came round here,' I said, trying to change the subject. 'What's the Great Bingo Caller in the Sky got for me today?'

He traced his finger down the chart, did some calculations and came to a decision. Putting his equipment aside, he shuffled some bones, burnt a joss stick and said in a voice of doom: 'I see great conflagration,' his fingers made flickering movements in my direction.

'As well as consternation?' I inquired.

'To be running concurrently,' he said, as if it were a jail sentence.

'Your ruler Venus is making an unfortunate aspect to Mars.'

'Oh! dear,' I said. 'Not again!'

'Be circumspect at all times and do not provoke the gods to anger.'

'Rightio, I'll be off, then,' I said, rummaging in my purse.

There was nobody in at home. I don't know what Mike and Heron are up to. They could be running a brothel or a gambling den. Suddenly I realized I had stopped caring. I was living from day to day, enjoying the sights and sounds and smells and wondering where the next meal was coming from, like a stray dog.

I walked along the beck through the Himalayan balsam, its seed capsules going snap, crackle and pop! like a bowl of Rice Krispies as I pushed past them. Round the back of Allen's mill, a secret hollow with yellow loosestrife and wild raspberries, the fruit just beginning to form; blue water forget-me-nots here and there in marshy clumps.

I picked a bunch of loosestrife and water mint to keep the flies away. Culpeper recommended it for nose bleeds; it may come in handy when I get home. I sat down for a minute and took out my diary.

11 August 2 AC
Dear Crispin woke me at cock-crow with a nosegay and a merry madrigal. He is away o'er the lea to help in the search for old Mr Bracken's Charolais bull. Harriet Hen has laid a freckled egg at my very door. Dear faithful friend, I will not forget you ere you go into the chicken chow mein. I gather mushrooms for our frugal repast, such a medley of sorts I scarce know what to do with them:

> A chanterelle
> You can sell,
> A blewit
> You can stew it.

My beloved borne home on a litter. He hath a great gore inflicted on his posterior. It seems he was bending to weave a garland to hang on the poor creature's neck, like Ferdinand, when he charged at him. His Party Popover lies close at hand with his favourite Wall's Choc Ice. He hath forgotten the kindling; he must needs go abroad tomorrow. Alack! but he cannot sit down anyway.

No sign of Otley in all this time. He will be back from the

hospital by now, whiling the hours away tickling trout or looking for badger tracks. He is a fritterer of the first water. It's time he got a job; but when they asked him what he wanted to do when he grew up he said, 'If I have to do something, I'll be a bird-watcher.' Then, when they said he'd have to get a proper job he said, 'I'll be a parson, then – they only work one day a week.' It's funny, though, when he's there I'm fed up with him, but when he's not there I think about him all the time – it must be love. We shall have to get a divorce and then phone each other every day like Taylor and Burton.

As I approached High Riding the smell of dinner cooking filtered through the shrubbery and I followed it like a Bisto kid. Thelma was in the kitchen laying the table: a basket of bread rolls, a dish of grated cheese, a bottle of spring water and a pot donkey full of pansies with 'A present from Cleethorpes' round its midriff.

'Oh! I'm sorry,' I lied, 'I've come at the wrong time.'

'You can stay if you like, there's plenty,' she said, her capable hands fluttering here and there like the butterflies they were so used to catching. Her black eyes fairly snapped with the excitement of organizing the garden party. Punch & Judy, obstacle races, coconut shies, throwing darts at Ronnie, Gorby and Maggie, a treasure hunt, ice-cream, treacle toffee and home-made scones. Did I think a pound was too much to charge? If we could get five hundred in that would be a tidy sum to add to the World Wildlife Fund. It might save a panda or two.

'We shall never get five hundred in here,' I said.

'We can do like they do at the zoo – let 'em in at one end and push 'em out the other,' she said.

'And it's bank holiday weekend, don't forget,' I cautioned.

'If they've got any sense at all they'll come up here instead of clogging the roads up with traffic jams. Stupid oafs,' she pronounced.

For an extra fifty pence she would throw open the house to the public and they could inspect her collection of Lepidoptera. A wall-map was displayed illustrating her travels, omitting any mention of that Corsican brigand she had spent the best part of ten years with; or the drunken rubber-planter in Malaya who went so far as to rub his wife out in a mad passion for the provocative, headstrong Thelma. 'She was my best friend,' Thelma told the judge. 'You could have knocked me down with a feather.' She kept her promise to send him food parcels, though.

By the time Sylvie came down with her knitting we were seated and listening to a Sibelius festival concert from the Free Trade Hall in Manchester. For a while a suitable hush was maintained, until Sylvie complained:

'I wanted to watch *Neighbours*.'

'Don't start that again or I'll wrap your bloody knitting round your neck,' Thelma said, as she dished out the fragrant moussaka.

'Is that the same scarf?' I asked conversationally.

'No, he wants two,' Sylvie said. 'One to wear and one in the wash.'

'I saw Jeff when I was up there on Sunday,' I said. 'He'll be back for the garden party.' Trying to cheer her up, poor soul. It'll be a shock when she knows I've gone back with him. Her blue eyes lit up like spring gentians in a sudden burst of sunlight.

'I shall never sleep till then,' she exclaimed.

'This moussaka's nice,' I complimented the chef. 'Is it made with TVP?' I had a packet and thought I might try it out later on.

'No, it's minced lamb. I'm getting anaemic with all this Third World stuff,' Thelma said, shovelling it down with relish.

'It might be radioactive, you know,' Sylvie pointed out, pushing her plate away and gulping a tumblerful of water.

Her sister's lips set in a determined line as she studiously looked out of the window.

'They're still testing for it and you know I don't like meat – you might have told me.' Sylvie twittered on like her Tinkerbell.

'Shut your gob!' said Thelma.

A bread-and-butter pudding followed made from Prince Charles's favourite recipe. I had not eaten so well for many weeks. Thelma turned the radio up as the resounding strains of 'Finlandia' lifted the roof off.

'Switch it off!' Sylvie screamed, clutching her forehead. 'It's giving me a headache; Big Daddies with their beards on banging and scraping away – I can't stand it.'

'Then go and put your head in the bloody fire-bucket!' Thelma shouted back, as Sylvie fled into the hall.

'Did you see *All Creatures Great and Small* the other night?' I asked politely. 'We watched them filming when we were up in the dales last year. Might even be on it for all we know.'

'Gave up watching it,' she said. 'They're forever up to the elbow in some animal's backside, and it's always when you're eating.'

I didn't know what to say next so I helped with the washing-up and tidied the kitchen. The afternoon sun lit up the old dresser searching out long forgotten corners: Thelma's butterflies; Granny Hawkweed's yellowing recipes; a tattered herbal; corks and bootlaces; buttons and bodkins; every drawer seemed to be full to overflowing. Then I noticed a small secret drawer, just big enough to hold my diary, behind the herbal. Full of dust and dead moths, it could never have been used. I cleaned it out and buried my treasure. It would be safe there from Otley's prying eyes. Only I would know where it was. The next two or three weeks would be busy ones getting ready for the garden party. Then I'd be off to the Moon. Otley would be searching for evidence. Well, he wouldn't find it.

'See you, then,' I called nonchalantly to Thelma as she changed out of her faded jungle print into her safari suit and fell-walkers. Sylvie waved from her bedroom window, Tinkerbell chirruping happily round her head. The lads were sprawled out on the lawn, a shadow of their former selves and very pleased, but hungry.

'Seen Jeff lately?' Bill called as I went past.

'He's gone down south dwyle-flonking,' I lied. 'He'll be back soon – didn't he tell you?'

'He flits up and down like Batman,' Wesley complained.

'We're forgetting all that tricky sticking,' said Chas.

How nice to get back to my little gingerbread house. A lump came into my throat at the thought of leaving it. I resolved to make a butterfly garden out of that squidgy cat-run going down into Hob Wood. And I'll never despise cabbages again. The Romans had a great admiration for them: they ate them and put them on their bad legs. I rolled up my jeans and examined my battered shins, wondering if it would work for me. I picked a large, juicy cabbage and dismantled it in the kitchen, tying the leaves round my legs with a piece of string. Sheer delight! and soon I was dozing in a shady corner of the wilderness.

I dreamt I was whizzing through the galaxy with Jeff, a row of silk cocoons hanging up on a silver clothes-line. After star-hopping to the tune of 'Waltzing Matilda', we landed on Earth.

'If we don't get some mulberry leaves quick they'll die,' Jeff said.

Then along came Julius Caesar with a cart-load of cabbages. 'Put them in here,' he said, 'they'll be all right.'

'Thanks a lot,' said Jeff. 'If you hop in we'll give you a lift down to the forum.'

'Haven't time,' said Caesar. 'I'm just off to invade Perfidious Albion.'

I was rudely interrupted by the master returning home

for his dinner. What did I think I was playing at? Was that all I had to do all day?

'I've been out all morning looking for you,' I said, 'and I called to see Mike but he wasn't in.'

'I went to Bradford for a change,' he said, 'and Mike went with me.'

THE NEXT TWO or three weeks passed pleasantly enough. A typical Pennine summer. The weather undecided between a cool, misty, Japanese brush-painting, or a hot, stifling, Rousseau junglescape. Otley even looked in the local paper for a job.

'There's one here for a Person Friday,' I told him, 'at the old nail factory; it's a boutique now.'

'That means they want a woman but they daren't say so,' he said.

'Why not?' I asked foolishly.

'Because they all want to be persons these days,' he sneered.

Another wanted to know if you were energetic, articulate and anxious to earn £500 a week with a company car.

'Double glazing salesman,' he said.

And another inquired if you were interested in health and would like to earn £100 a week working only in your spare time.

'Pyramid selling,' said Otley. 'American slimming pills that don't work – they'll be on *That's Life* next year.'

A trainee pattern-cutter wanted, with an opportunity to invest in the family business. That sounded all right.

'Asian sweat-shop,' he said. 'You'll be shut in a dark cellar all day like a lot of cockroaches.'

A school caretaker at the new comprehensive in Quarry Bottoms?

'They won't employ you if you're a war hero with a pension,' he said. 'They want the jobs to go to the destitute.'

In the end he decided to apply for the job of social worker in London where he would not be discriminated against on account of age, sex, race, religion, disabilities or criminal record. He would be free after the garden party, he told them.

We managed to persuade Mike to put 'Silver Riding' on tape so that there was no danger of us all being electrocuted by wet live cables lurking in the bushes. Hope he won't be wearing his Nazi uniform.

I packed my case one night when Otley was watching *Equinox* – a programme about computers. I hope he picks up a few tips on how to be user-friendly. Toothbrush, Kleenex, drip-dry frock, Kendal mint cake, safety pins, cardigan, support stockings, magic pen. I can borrow a kangaroo suit when I get there.

We had the garden party on the Sunday because Thelma didn't want the chapel lot coming in spoiling the fun.

'Po-faced misery guts,' she said, 'looking as farl as pot mules and sucking their mint humbugs.'

It was a bright sunny day; and it was raining in Spain, the news said, which cheered everybody up. All those people paying all that money to lug heavy suitcases to the Costa del Sol – ha! ha! ha! – the silly sods! Serves 'em right!

'It's that hole in the ozone layer,' Otley said. 'It's thrown everything to cock.'

'I know,' said Sylvie.

'Get a move on!' Thelma shouted, clapping her hands as if we were coolies. Soon all the tables and stalls were set out. Brandy snaps, sausage rolls, sticky buns, ginger-beer; and Mrs Depledge installed behind the tea-urn like the Metropolitan of Moscow behind a samovar.

One of the first to arrive was Tinker Sly with his shotgun looking for his £5 which I had clean forgot.

'Be off with you!' Otley said. 'It's only fifteen pence with a Metro Permit.'

'I promised him,' I said, looking in my handbag. 'Can I borrow it off you? I've only got two fifty-pence pieces and a fourpenny stamp.'

'Bloody Shylock!' he grumbled, as he handed it over. 'And mind you draw it out of the Post Office on Tuesday,' he said, turning to me.

When he wasn't watching I sneaked my case into the bushes down by the summer house. Jeff said that the Kraak would land after dusk on the back lawn leading up to the east wing. Everybody would scream and run away, he said, giving me time to snatch my case and get aboard. Steve had come down, as well, to fetch Gordon. I thought I saw him whispering to Otley at one point; I hope he told him that Mickey and Minnie had been adopted by a caring family who sing and dance with their children every night and read them a bedtime story instead of watching *Sporting Triangles*.

Jeff and Sylvie won the three-legged race by a mile. Her eyes shone like the blue lamp on top of an ambulance.

'He's electric!' she said afterwards. Poor soul.

Old Mrs Sidebottom won the sack-race. She's used to jumping about at home in one of those foot-muffs. Little Marjorie Briggs with her fat orange curls screamed blue murder and was bundled out by her red-faced mother. Sounds of smacking echoed through the ginnels as they made their way home.

Soon it was time for the morris dancing and Otley appeared in his baldric and bells. They danced on trestle tables laid on the grass, as they like to make a lot of noise. 'Swaggering Boney' first as they had to do a lot of leap-frogging about. 'Nancy's Fancy', 'The Nutting Girl', 'The Monks' March', and then the fertility dance. They're sex maniacs!

'Not the 'earole, not the 'earole,' Jeff reminded them.

'Young Collins' to finish with as they were dying for a pint.

'Remember the tricky sticking,' their leader called. 'We want no more black eyes and broken noses.'

Otley sank to the ground beside me, sweat running off the end of his chin, daisies and buttercups hanging loose off his hat, with the fury of the stamping and twirling. If only he would put so much energy into getting a job! We could be rich beyond the dreams of avarice.

'I'm sticking to bird-watching in future,' he decided.

I mopped his brow with a piece of paper tablecloth blown into my lap by a sudden breeze. I fetched some tea and sandwiches and we ate them leaning against a lump of granite that sparkled like diamonds in the sunlight. Jeff winked as he went by with the lads carrying the tables away, Thelma clapping them on and Sylvie trailing behind.

'You ought to give them a hand,' I said, shamefaced.

'I'm knackered,' my hero said.

Gales of laughter coming from the peasantry throwing darts at Ronnie, Gorby and Maggie. Frowns of disapproval from the high-minded who write to *The Times* complaining about *Spitting Image*. A lull when the hour of limbo struck and then a buzz of activity as they all rushed home to watch *Surprise Surprise*. Soon the night-hunters began to arrive – roving-eyed youths with earrings and cans of brown ale, pursued by a pack of barking dogs.

'Gerrardavit,' Otley growled, laying about them with a stick.

'Remember we're here to help save the animals,' I told him.

'That's *world* wildlife,' he said, throwing stones at a straggler. 'We don't want every dog in the neighbourhood shitting on the lawn.'

'Sh! Don't be so vulgar,' I hissed. That genteel Mrs Smythe-Knowles was sitting nearby giving her hairdo a squirt of lacquer and wiping her fingers on eau-de-Cologne fresh-ups. What she would think of him, I do not know. I'm glad I'm going to the Moon now. I picked up my plastic mac and my handbag and stormed off into the kitchen to help with the washing-up. Standing knee-deep in debris and surrounded by matching red-and-white picnic plates and mugs, the workers sweated in a cloud of steam. I joined them in a blazing temper and attacked the pile of plates, sending fairy bubbles flying in all directions. We had finished in no time at all and my companions then stuffed tea-cakes, buns and sausage rolls into their carrier bags and made off with them.

'Here you are,' said the head washer-upper. 'Put these tea-cakes in your bag or those buggers'll take 'em all.'

When the kitchen was cleared I pushed through a crowd of small boys waiting to see the Lepidoptera and Sylvie came down dressed as a governess ready to sing 'Shall We Dance?' Bert Aldridge made a passable king and pulled his eyes up with Sellotape. The little Gujaratis sang 'Getting to Know You' and then ran off into the bushes squawking like parrots, their mothers after them firing words as if they were bullets from a machine-gun.

The sun went down and I hid behind a rhododendron when Otley came into view. He seemed to be looking for somebody. Bella, I expect. Shortly the music struck up for dancing. Mr Scattergood's record player plugged into an extension reel.

'Here's one or two for the old 'uns,' he announced. 'Join

in if you know the words.' His whiskers parted as he opened his mouth to sing.

'Red sails in the sunset,' he warbled, and the youngsters burst out laughing. The tree lights came on and dapper Mr Fairburn with his patent-leather hair danced by with Miss Armitage. Otley dodged out of the way when he saw her in case she wanted to give him some marriage guidance. Soon they were all shuffling round the lawn.

'Marcheta, Marcheta,' sang one of the old records rescued from the Oxfam shop, like a ghost from the past. Then Mr Scattergood played Great-Aunt Jane's favourite, a sultry Argentine tango but I remember we kids used to put our own words to it.

'Oh! Donna Clara, I saw your bloomers last night!' we sang, as we marched down the lane ten abreast going to the chip shop. Happy days! I longed to join in but I dared not reveal myself. The young were getting restless and somebody plugged in some disco lights, the scene changing to red, blue, gold, green and violet, in quick succession.

'We want Johnny Rotten!' they began to chant.

'You'll be old yourself one day,' Mr Scattergood warned them.

In the confusion I hadn't noticed the flying saucer land until I heard a whirring noise coming from behind the trees and I saw the Kraak perched on one of the top branches examining a Chinese lantern. He couldn't land on the crowded lawn. What would they do now? And where was Jeff? I would have to find him somehow. I picked up my case and began to creep round the lawn keeping in the bushes. Thank goodness I was travelling light. Round by the compost heap. Old wood stacked waiting for a bonfire by a rickety shed. Thick ivy suffocating the walls of the house. Bags of rubbish waiting for collection, cardboard boxes and waxed cartons spilling over everywhere. It'll soon be like this on the Moon. I'm glad I shall see it while it's still virgin.

The dancers were still slowly spinning like Fortune's Wheel hypnotized now by memories of yore. Rugged faces grew suddenly soft.

'Get 'em off!' chanted the yobbos.

Then Mike appeared with his tapes and a great cheer went up.

'Erewiggo, erewiggo, erewiggo! Erewiggo, erewiggo, erewiggo-o!' They chanted as he plugged in his adaptor.

The Master of Ceremonies held up his arms for silence and there was an expectant hush. 'Ladies and gentlemen, we thank you most sincerely for giving generously to the World Wildlife Fund, and His Worship the Mayor . . .'

'Get on with it,' they chanted, forcing him to cut his speech short.

'And it is my pleasure to present to you the world première of our very own song, "Silver Riding", composed by a young lad you all know – here he is, folks – Michael Craven!'

I was so proud of Mike I rushed out of hiding to give him a hug. Then everything happened at once. At the first explosion from Mike's ghetto-blaster the Kraak flew screeching back to the skimmer and started the take-off lights flashing. Jeff came running across the lawn from nowhere and then Steve, carrying a wriggling holdall, joined him from behind the summer house. I snatched up my case and followed them.

'Wait for me; I'm here,' I called.

Then an assailant overpowered me, flung me to the ground and tied my hands behind my back.

'Hurry up!' Jeff called out. 'We have lift-off!'

'That's my wife!' Otley shouted. 'I'll have you up for en-ticement.'

Something was tied round my mouth and I was lifted to my feet, Otley on one side and Percy from the Neighbour-hood Watch on the other. While they're doing this, people's houses are getting burgled.

By now the saucer was ready for taking off; High Riding was lit up as if by a megaton bomb with everybody looking on, astonished, as they had at the fireworks display on the Queen's Jubilee. I struggled to free myself but was gripped in a vice and could only watch helplessly. It was getting hotter and the tree-tops began to sizzle, the ground a shimmering haze like the one Omar Sharif came out of to meet Lawrence of Arabia.

'We're off, then,' Jeff yelled, above the noise. I tried to call out.

Then Sylvie rushed forward, all dressed up in one of Thelma's safari suits, a Doctor Who scarf round her neck and Tinkerbell in his cage, flapping his wings excitedly and scattering Chirrupy bird-seed in all directions. Thelma came hot on her heels, but Sylvie sprinted ahead.

'Wait a minute!' she screamed. 'I had to go back for Tinkie!'

'Get in, then, we haven't got any bluebirds,' said Jeff, delighted.

'You've got my best suit on,' shouted Thelma frantically.

Sylvie stopped in her tracks as if she had suddenly remembered something important; the ends of her scarf were beginning to catch fire.

'Charlton Heston's not up there with his tablets, is he?' she inquired.

'Go on, get in, if you're going,' said Thelma, giving her a violent push.

A whoosh! and they were gone, sending out a sheet of flame over the piled-up rubbish by the woodshed; the bonfire sticks caught alight and set fire to the old ivy roots and in no time at all the house was ablaze. The fire brigade was soon on the scene. My hands were untied and we all pitched in getting water wherever we could find it and making gallons of strong, sweet tea. When the fire was under control we rested to gather strength before going home and I reflected on the irony that now the windows had been cleaned Sylvie wasn't here to see it.

Mr Fairburn volunteered to stay and comfort Thelma. 'You'll be needing a hand,' he said, casting an expert eye over the premises. He was an estate agent.

Sammy Chandra ran his extended family home in six shifts and then came back to pick us up. The three of us, dishevelled and begrimed, sank into the back seat: Mike with his earphones on, jigging up and down to his Sony Walkman; Otley with a smirk and me with a splitting headache.

'It was a complete re-enactment of the *Ramayana*!' exclaimed Sammy, 'and such decisiveness is entirely unexpected in one born on the cusp.'

The first pale green light of dawn showed on the horizon as we sped down the hill, leaving High Riding smouldering like a rumbling volcano. It was good to be home. I'd had enough of this do-it-yourself stuff. But what were those bags doing packed and waiting by the front door?

'Where's Heron?' I asked.

'He's gone,' said Mike.

'Gone where?' I said fearfully. Mike was hiding something.

'I dunno,' he said.

'He's gone to San Francisco, hasn't he?' I demanded. 'And you're going to join him.'

'Why would we want to go to San Francisco?' he laughed.

'Er . . . to see the Golden Gate,' I said, with great presence of mind. 'That's your bags packed, isn't it?'

'Yes,' he said, as bold as brass, the young scallywag!

'We shall never see you again if you go there,' I blurted out.

'Actually,' he said, 'I'm going to Skegness with Pauline before we go back to the tech. She's fed up with being a boy – she wants a change.'

Thank God! I'm going to get some posterity after all. I made some scrambled eggs and coffee and we gobbled them down like a pack of wolves. Then I sank into a squashy chair while Otley lay on the sofa.

'Don't put your dirty feet up on the furniture,' I complained.

'Get stuffed!' he said. 'I'm knackered.'

'Now, look here,' said Mike, 'I'm just about fed up with you two – it's time we had some *perestroika* round here.'

'*Perestroika*?' I inquired, in the middle of a yawn. He was tiresome.

'And *glasnost*,' he went on. It seemed he was ashamed of us, showing him up all the time in front of the yobs. So we agreed to mend our ways; Otley made a slashing noise across his throat and turned on Radio Leeds.

'The fire brigade was called out to deal with a house fire at High Riding last night,' the newsreader informed us, as if we didn't know. 'No one was hurt and the damage was confined to the kitchen and the east wing. It is thought the fire was started by a carelessly discarded cigarette end.'

'They always say that,' said Otley. 'They think we're stupid.'

The kitchen, the newsreader said. Oh my God! My diary was in the kitchen dresser.

'My diary!' I said, leaping to my feet. 'My life's work.'

'What about it?' asked Mike. Otley was no longer interested: Steve had told him the truth about Crispin so he was satisfied that I wasn't really a bawdy-basket. He could go back to not caring about me again.

'It's burnt!' I sobbed. 'I left it in the kitchen at the Big House, I was afraid you might tear it up.'

'Bloody good job too. That's what you call poetic justice,' said Otley.

'Never mind,' Mike said, putting his arm round my

shoulders, 'you can easy do another one; I'll give you one of my books.'

'Thanks,' I sobbed. He wasn't such a bad scallywag, after all.

'And make sure you put me in it next time,' said my beloved husband, lolling about like the Wali of Swat. 'It's one of my conjugal rights.'

Baldrics! I thought to myself. Go and get 'em round the pub.

'All right, then,' I lied.

FOR THE BEST IN PAPERBACKS, LOOK FOR THE

In every corner of the world, on every subject under the sun, Penguin represents quality and variety – the very best in publishing today.

For complete information about books available from Penguin – including Puffins, Penguin Classics and Arkana – and how to order them, write to us at the appropriate address below. Please note that for copyright reasons the selection of books varies from country to country.

In the United Kingdom: Please write to *Dept E.P., Penguin Books Ltd, Harmondsworth, Middlesex, UB7 0DA.*

If you have any difficulty in obtaining a title, please send your order with the correct money, plus ten per cent for postage and packaging, to *PO Box No 11, West Drayton, Middlesex*

In the United States: Please write to *Dept BA, Penguin, 299 Murray Hill Parkway, East Rutherford, New Jersey 07073*

In Canada: Please write to *Penguin Books Canada Ltd, 2801 John Street, Markham, Ontario L3R 1B4*

In Australia: Please write to the *Marketing Department, Penguin Books Australia Ltd, P.O. Box 257, Ringwood, Victoria 3134*

In New Zealand: Please write to the *Marketing Department, Penguin Books (NZ) Ltd, Private Bag, Takapuna, Auckland 9*

In India: Please write to *Penguin Overseas Ltd, 706 Eros Apartments, 56 Nehru Place, New Delhi, 110019*

In the Netherlands: Please write to *Penguin Books Netherlands B.V., Postbus 195, NL–1380AD Weesp*

In West Germany: Please write to *Penguin Books Ltd, Friedrichstrasse 10–12, D–6000 Frankfurt/Main 1*

In Spain: Please write to *Longman Penguin España, Calle San Nicolas 15, E–28013 Madrid*

In Italy: Please write to *Penguin Italia s.r.l., Via Como 4, I-20096 Pioltello (Milano)*

In France: Please write to *Penguin Books Ltd, 39 Rue de Montmorency, F-75003 Paris*

In Japan: Please write to *Longman Penguin Japan Co Ltd, Yamaguchi Building, 2–12–9 Kanda Jimbocho, Chiyoda-Ku, Tokyo 101*

PENGUIN BESTSELLERS

The New Confessions William Boyd

The outrageous, hilarious autobiography of John James Todd, a Scotsman born in 1899 and one of the great self-appointed (and failed) geniuses of the twentieth century. 'Brilliant ... a Citizen Kane of a novel' – *Daily Telegraph*

The House of Stairs Barbara Vine

'A masterly and hypnotic synthesis of past, present and terrifying future ... compelling and disturbing' – *Sunday Times*. 'Not only ... a quietly smouldering suspense novel but also ... an accurately atmospheric portrayal of London in the heady '60s. Literally unputdownable' – *Time Out*

Summer's Lease John Mortimer

'It's high summer, high comedy too, when Molly drags her amiably bickering family to a rented Tuscan villa for the hols ... With a cosy fluency of wit, Mortimer charms us into his urbane tangle of clues...' – *Mail on Sunday*. 'Superb' – Ruth Rendell

Touch Elmore Leonard

'I bleed from five wounds and heal people, but I've never been in love. Isn't that something?' They call him Juvenal, and he's a wanted man in downtown Detroit... 'Discover Leonard for yourself – he's something else' – *Daily Mail*

Story of My Life Jay McInerney

'The first year I was in New York I didn't do anything but guys and blow...' 'The leader of the pack' – *Time Out*. 'Fast and sharp ... a very good novel indeed' – *Observer*

FOR THE BEST IN PAPERBACKS, LOOK FOR THE 🐧

PENGUIN BESTSELLERS

Riding the Iron Rooster Paul Theroux

An eye-opening and entertaining account of travels in old and new China, from the author of *The Great Railway Bazaar*. 'Mr Theroux cannot write badly … in the course of a year there was almost no train in the vast Chinese rail network on which he did not travel' – Ludovic Kennedy

Touched by Angels Derek Jameson

His greatest story yet – his own. 'My story is simple enough. I grew up poor and hungry on the streets of London's East End and decided at an early age it was better to be rich and successful.'

The Rich are Different Susan Howatch

Wealth is power – and all power corrupts. 'A superb saga, with all the bestselling ingredients – love, hate, death, murder, and a hell of a lot of passion' – *Daily Mirror*

The Cold Moons Aeron Clement

For a hundred generations the badgers of Cilgwyn had lived in harmony with nature – until a dying stranger limped into their midst, warning of the coming of men. Men whose scent had inexplicably terrified him, men armed with rifles and poison gas…

The Return of Heroic Failures Stephen Pile

The runaway success of *The Book of Heroic Failures* was a severe embarrassment to its author. From the song-free Korean version of *The Sound of Music* to the least successful attempt to tranquillize an animal, his hilarious sequel plumbs new depths of human incompetence.

The Unabashed Alex Charles Peattie and Russell Taylor

Alex is the *Independent*'s daily strip-cartoon. With its characters drawn from every tax bracket – bullish Alex, bearish Clive, decidedly boorish Vince and their yuppie molls – and its lowdown on the downside of today's wealth generation, it chronicles the City's most exciting era ever.

Un Four-Pack de Franglais Miles Kington

Les quatre hilarious volumes de Franglais dans one mind-boggling livre! Avec cet omnibus vous pouvez relax avec le knowledge que vous won't be stuck for quelque chose à dire anywhere in the Franglais-speaking monde, et cope avec any situation, n'importe quoi, either side de la Manche, or even in it.

Milligan's War Spike Milligan

The best bits of the greatest war memoirs in the English language in one volume, featuring Harry Secombe, crabs, the dreaded Cold Collation and Spike's underwear collection as just a few of the secret weapons that won the war. 'Desperately funny' – *Sunday Times*

Imitations of Immortality E. O. Parrott

A dazzling and witty selection of imitative verse and prose as immortal as the writers and the works they seek to parody. 'Immensely funny' – *The Times Educational Supplement*. 'The richest literary plum-pie ever confected ... One will return to it again and again' – Arthur Marshall

How to be a Brit George Mikes

This George Mikes omnibus contains *How to be an Alien*, *How to be Inimitable* and *How to be Decadent*, three volumes of invaluable research for those not lucky enough to have been born British and who would like to make up for this deficiency. Even the born-and-bred Brit can learn a thing or two from the insights George Mikes offers here.

Wuthering Depths

Bette Howell's gloriously cheeky and entertaining send-up of English village life.

Plans are afoot to turn the Mill House – Wuthering Depths to the locals – into an international tourist attraction. Meanwhile the Hawkweeds are in their usual chaos – Freda dreaming of Torremolinos, ancient Cousin Myrtle donning her boots for the next Greenpeace rally, mad Ottley pacing the moors in search of spies and his wife May succumbing to the charms of handsome Kit Constable, the village Michaelangelo . . .

Romantic Brontëland? Forget it. *Wuthering Depths* tells of life at Low Riding as it really is!

'Charmingly idiosyncratic and original . . . a whimsical and humorous look at the less-romantic passions which occupy the energies of modern-day Yorkshire folk' – *Yorkshire Post*

'A benign and witty exploration of that compelling fictional area where anarchy and domesticity meet . . . Betty Howell has a sure hand' – Fay Weldon